NECKLACE

Wish Pendant

A Wish Pendant is worn by a Wish-Granter and can be anything from a necklace to a bracelet to eyeglasses. On Wishworld, these Wish Pendants help the Star Darlings identify their Wishers and store the ever-important wish energy.

LAVENDERITE

Power Crystal

Once a Star Darling has granted her first wish and returns to Starland, she receives a very special treasure—a beautiful Power Crystal.

Sage and the Journey
to Wishworld

Shana Muldoon Zappa and Ahmet Zappa

with Zelda Rose

Disney Press

Los Angeles • New York

Printed in the United States of America
Reinforced Binding
First Edition, September 2015
1 3 5 7 9 10 8 6 4 2

FAC-029261-15212

Library of Congress Cataloging-in-Publication Data
Zappa, Shana Muldoon.
Sage and the Journey to Wishworld/by Shana Muldoon Zappa
& Ahmet Zappa; with Zelda Rose.—First edition.
pages cm.—(Star Darlings; [1])
ISBN 978-1-4231-6643-6
[1. Wishes—Fiction. 2. Stars—Fiction. 3. Schools—Fiction.
4. Science fiction.] I. Zappa, Ahmet. II. Rose, Zelda.
III. Title.
pz7.z2582We 2013
[Fic]—dc   232012048279

For more Disney Press fun, visit www.disneybooks.com

SUSTAINABLE
FORESTRY
INITIATIVE

Certified Chain of Custody
Promoting Sustainable Forestry

www.sfiprogram.org
SFI-01054

The SFI label applies to the text stock

To our beautiful, sweet treasure,
Halo Violetta Zappa. You are pure light and joy
and our greatest inspiration. We love you soooo much.

May every step upon your path be blessed with positivity and
the understanding that you have the power within you to
manifest the most fulfilling life you can possibly imagine and
more. May you always remember that being different and true
to your highest self makes your inner star shine brighter.

Remember that you have the power of choice. . . . Choose thoughts
that feel good. Choose love and friendship that feed your spirit.
Choose actions for peace and nourishment. Choose boundaries
for the same. Choose what speaks to your creativity and unique
inner voice . . . what truly makes you happy. And always know
that no matter what you choose, you are unconditionally loved.

Look up to the stars and know you are never alone.
When in doubt, go within . . . the answers are all there.
Smiles light the world and laughter is the best medicine.
And NEVER EVER stop making wishes. . . .

Glow for it. . . .
Mommy and Daddy

And to everyone else here on "Wishworld":

May you realize that no matter where you are in life, no
matter what you look like or where you were born, you, too,
have the power within you to create the life of your dreams.
Through celebrating your own uniqueness, thinking positively,
and taking action, you can make your wishes come true.

Smile. The Star Darlings have your back.
We know how startastic you truly are.

Glow for it. . . .
Your friends,
Shana and Ahmet

Student Reports

NAME: Clover
BRIGHT DAY: January 5
FAVORITE COLOR: Purple
INTERESTS: Music, painting, studying
WISH: To be the best songwriter and DJ on Starland
WHY CHOSEN: Clover has great self-discipline, patience, and willpower. She is creative, responsible, dependable, and extremely loyal.
WATCH OUT FOR: Clover can be hard to read and she is reserved with those she doesn't know. She's afraid to take risks and can be a wisecracker at times.
SCHOOL YEAR: Second
POWER CRYSTAL: Panthera
WISH PENDANT: Barrette

NAME: Adora
BRIGHT DAY: February 14
FAVORITE COLOR: Sky blue
INTERESTS: Science, thinking about the future and how she can make it better
WISH: To be the top fashion designer on Starland
WHY CHOSEN: Adora is clever and popular and cares about the world around her. She's a deep thinker.
WATCH OUT FOR: Adora can have her head in the clouds and be thinking about other things.
SCHOOL YEAR: Third
POWER CRYSTAL: Azurica
WISH PENDANT: Watch

NAME: Piper
BRIGHT DAY: March 4
FAVORITE COLOR: Seafoam green
INTERESTS: Composing poetry and writing in her dream journal
WISH: To become the best version of herself she can possibly be and to share that by writing books
WHY CHOSEN: Piper is giving, kind, and sensitive. She is very intuitive and aware.
WATCH OUT FOR: Piper can be dreamy, absentminded, and wishy-washy. She can also be moody and easily swayed by the opinions of others.
SCHOOL YEAR: Second
POWER CRYSTAL: Dreamalite
WISH PENDANT: Bracelets

Starling Academy

NAME: Astra
BRIGHT DAY: April 9
FAVORITE COLOR: Red
INTERESTS: Individual sports
WISH: To be the best athlete on Starland—to win!
WHY CHOSEN: Astra is energetic, brave, clever, and confident. She has boundless energy and is always direct and to the point.
WATCH OUT FOR: Astra is sometimes cocky, self-centered, condescending, and brash.
SCHOOL YEAR: Second
POWER CRYSTAL: Quarrelite
WISH PENDANT: Wristbands

* · · * · · * · · * · · *

NAME: Tessa
BRIGHT DAY: May 18
FAVORITE COLOR: Emerald green
INTERESTS: Food, flowers, love
WISH: To be successful enough so she can enjoy a life of luxury
WHY CHOSEN: Tessa is warm, charming, affectionate, trustworthy, and dependable. She has incredible drive and commitment.
WATCH OUT FOR: Tessa does not like to be rushed. She can be quite stubborn and often says no. She does not deal well with change and is prone to exaggeration. She can be easily sidetracked.
SCHOOL YEAR: Third
POWER CRYSTAL: Gossamer
WISH PENDANT: Brooch

* · · * · · * · · * · · *

NAME: Gemma
BRIGHT DAY: June 2
FAVORITE COLOR: Orange
INTERESTS: Sharing her thoughts about almost anything
WISH: To be valued for her opinions on everything
WHY CHOSEN: Gemma is friendly, easygoing, funny, extroverted, and social. She knows a little bit about everything.
WATCH OUT FOR: Gemma talks—a lot—and can be a little too honest sometimes and offend others. She can have a short attention span and can be superficial.
SCHOOL YEAR: First
POWER CRYSTAL: Scatterite
WISH PENDANT: Earrings

Student Reports

NAME: Cassie
BRIGHT DAY: July 6
FAVORITE COLOR: White
INTERESTS: Reading, crafting
WISH: To be more independent and confident and less fearful
WHY CHOSEN: Cassie is extremely imaginative and artistic. She is a voracious reader and is loyal, caring, and a good friend. She is very intuitive.
WATCH OUT FOR: Cassie can be distrustful, jealous, moody, and brooding.
SCHOOL YEAR: First
POWER CRYSTAL: Lunalite
WISH PENDANT: Glasses

⋆⋆⋆⋆⋆⋆★⋆⋆⋆⋆⋆⋆

NAME: Leona
BRIGHT DAY: August 16
FAVORITE COLOR: Gold
INTERESTS: Acting, performing, dressing up
WISH: To be the most famous pop star on Starland
WHY CHOSEN: Leona is confident, hardworking, generous, open-minded, optimistic, caring, and a strong leader.
WATCH OUT FOR: Leona can be vain, opinionated, selfish, bossy, dramatic, and stubborn and is prone to losing her temper.
SCHOOL YEAR: Third
POWER CRYSTAL: Glisten paw
WISH PENDANT: Cuff

⋆⋆⋆⋆⋆⋆★⋆⋆⋆⋆⋆⋆

NAME: Vega
BRIGHT DAY: September 1
FAVORITE COLOR: Blue
INTERESTS: Exercising, analyzing, cleaning, solving puzzles
WISH: To be the top student at Starling Academy
WHY CHOSEN: Vega is reliable, observant, organized, and very focused.
WATCH OUT FOR: Vega can be opinionated about everything, and she can be fussy, uptight, critical, arrogant, and easily embarrassed.
SCHOOL YEAR: Second
POWER CRYSTAL: Queezle
WISH PENDANT: Belt

Starling Academy

NAME: Libby
BRIGHT DAY: October 12
FAVORITE COLOR: Pink
INTERESTS: Helping others, interior design, art, dancing
WISH: To give everyone what they need—both on Starland and through wish granting on Wishworld
WHY CHOSEN: Libby is generous, articulate, gracious, diplomatic, and kind.
WATCH OUT FOR: Libby can be indecisive and may try too hard to please everyone.
SCHOOL YEAR: First
POWER CRYSTAL: Charmelite
WISH PENDANT: Necklace

* • • * • • * • • * • • *

NAME: Scarlet
BRIGHT DAY: November 3
FAVORITE COLOR: Black
INTERESTS: Crystal climbing (and other extreme sports), magic, thrill seeking
WISH: To live on Wishworld
WHY CHOSEN: Scarlet is confident, intense, passionate, magnetic, curious, and very brave.
WATCH OUT FOR: Scarlet is a loner and can alienate others by being secretive, arrogant, stubborn, and jealous.
SCHOOL YEAR: Third
POWER CRYSTAL: Ravenstone
WISH PENDANT: Boots

* • • * • • * • • * • • *

NAME: Sage
BRIGHT DAY: December 1
FAVORITE COLOR: Lavender
INTERESTS: Travel, adventure, telling stories, nature, and philosophy
WISH: To become the best Wish-Granter Starland has ever seen
WHY CHOSEN: Sage is honest, adventurous, curious, optimistic, friendly, and relaxed.
WATCH OUT FOR: Sage has a quick temper! She can also be restless, irresponsible, and too trusting of others' opinions. She may jump to conclusions.
SCHOOL YEAR: First
POWER CRYSTAL: Lavenderite
WISH PENDANT: Necklace

Prologue

"Are we there yet?" Sage asked eagerly.

The only answer was a loud snore from Sage's father, Leonard. As soon as he had programmed the coordinates into their Starcar's console, he had fallen sound asleep—as usual. Sage's mom, Indirra, didn't even look up from her reading. That, too, was usual. Sage thought her mother should have been the one who was nodding off, as she was deep in a scientific holo-journal. But as one of Starland's leading research scientists, she found it engrossing. Luckily, Indirra didn't take her daughter's lack of interest in her chosen field as an insult; rather, she took it as a challenge.

Sage's seven-year-old twin brothers, Archer and Helio, paid no attention, either. They sat cross-legged on the floor, cheering on their cyber-wrestlers, which were engaged in a fierce battle. "Pin him! Pin him!" they yelled in support of their opposing fighters.

Sage stared at her family. *How can they be so blasé?* she wondered. It was no ordinary day. It was, actually, the most exciting day of her life! She leaned toward the dashboard and lifted a finger, letting it hover over the hyper-speed button. Should she press it? Suddenly, her hand was gently slapped away by her ever-watchful grandmother, a tough old lady everyone called Gran, who then uttered the words Sage had been hearing since she was a tiny Starling.

"Patience, Sage," she said.

Sage rolled her eyes. "You know I don't have any," she responded. Sage smiled sweetly at her grandmother before she added, "Just like you."

Gran shrugged and handed Sage a wrapped candy from her large purse. Sage popped the candy into her mouth and promptly spat it out. Moonberry. Dis-*gus*-ting. Sage sighed and glanced out the window. She caught a glimpse of her reflection. Slightly sparkly skin, just like all Starlings had. Long, thick glimmering lavender hair hanging in braids that nearly reached her waist. A pointy chin and large twinkling violet eyes that gave her a slightly mischievous look. Cheeks permanently flushed pink. Rosebud lips that were usually curved into a playful smile but were drawn into an irritated frown at the moment. The car was traveling so quickly that the scenery was one big blur. But to Sage, it felt like they were going in slow motion. She just wanted to get there already!

Finally, when Sage thought she might scream, they were almost there. She looked out the window and gasped. The long, straight road that led to the gates of her brand-new boarding school was lined with towering trees, their spindly branches covered in brilliant lavender blooms. The branches stretched up into a tangled canopy overhead, forming a colorful tunnel that led to the entrance.

Gran spoke, startling Sage. "Kaleidoscope trees," she told her granddaughter. "I haven't seen those since I was a young girl. They're quite rare. I forgot how beautiful they are. Keep watching—they'll change color." Sure enough, the blossoms began to turn a cheerful shade of pink before their eyes.

"Starmendous," said Sage. "I wonder how they change color like that."

"It's because they are composed of ninety-four percent iridusvapor," said Sage's mom without looking up. "Of course."

Sage and Gran exchanged grins. Indirra never missed an opportunity to share scientific information with her family. Her powers of concentration were a family legend. Once she had held a holo-conference call while the twins, convinced they needed to bathe their pet glowfur, chased it all around the house, wreaking havoc around her. She hadn't even seemed to notice. But Gran more than made up for that with her constant attention to detail and her habit of stating the obvious.

The car hovered up to the high black iron gates, which had an oddly lovely design of delicate curlicues and dangerously sharp spikes. Beyond them lay the campus of Starling Academy. Sage caught a quick glimpse of neat walkways, hedges trimmed into whimsical shapes, glittering buildings, and a lone white tower reaching high into the sky. The school, on the outskirts of Starland City, the largest metropolis on Starland, had an enviable location. The campus was near the violet-hued Luminous Lake and the stunning Crystal Mountains. The breathtaking site had inspired students for hydrongs of staryears. In the distance Sage could see the mountains in all their multicolored glory. The clouds parted and a beam of sunlight broke through, lighting up the campus with a rainbow glow while transforming the low-lying clouds into delicate spun-sugar confections. Sage shook her head. She was excited to finally be at Starling Academy, and it was almost too much to take in at once. She was superbly, stupendously, starmendously excited. That was what she had been working so hard for. Nothing was going to stop her now.

The gates rolled open slowly and the car inched forward, then came to a stop in front of a small glass booth. A Bot-Bot guard appeared and held up a hand scanner. The Starcar's window lowered, and without a moment's hesitation, Sage reached out and placed her palm on the scanner. It lit up bright blue. Accepted.

"Welcome to Starling Academy, Sage," the guard said. It handed her a holo-book.

She took it and replied, "Star salutations," the traditional Starling thank-you. She gave the Bot-Bot guard a friendly wave, which, as expected, was not returned. Her little brothers broke into peals of laughter at the clipped cybernetic voice. "Welcome. To. Starling. Academy. Sage," they echoed.

Gran looked over her shoulder. "It's the Student Manual," she whispered.

"Are you sure?" Sage replied, pointing to the on-screen title. "I thought it was the cafeteria menu."

"Fresh," said Gran, mock seriously.

Sage loved her grandmother fiercely but also liked to tease her. Fortunately, Gran liked to give as good as she could take.

Sage's mom shut off her holo-journal and looked around at everyone, blinking slowly. "Are we here already?" she asked brightly.

Sage rolled her eyes. "Yes, Mom," she said.

Sage's father startled awake with a loud snort. "What—who—where am I?" he sputtered. That sent the boys on another round of giggles.

Sage ignored them. She looked around, took a deep breath, and squinched her eyes closed as the car glided through the entrance and the gates rolled shut behind them. She could really picture herself happy there. *I wish for big, exciting things to happen to me here*, she thought.

Her wish would come true.

And then some.

CHAPTER
1

"Good afternoon, Miss Sage. Are you ready to begin your tour?"

Sage spun around.

"Up here," the voice said.

Sage craned her neck. Hovering in the air over her family members' heads was a medium-sized metallic orb. It flashed in the sunlight, forcing Sage to look away.

"What *is* that thing?" Gran asked, shielding her eyes and squinting.

"It's a floating Bot-Bot guide," explained Sage's father. "The neighbors hired one on their trip to Booshel Bay. They're supposed to be quite informative."

"Affirmative," said the Bot-Bot guide in its clipped tone. The boys giggled, but a stern look from Gran shushed them. "I am MO-J4 and I am quite informative, if I do say so myself." He blinked when he spoke.

"So can we go to the dorm now?" Sage asked.

The Bot-Bot guide paused, apparently running the request through his program to determine its validity. "Negative," he answered. "Before you head to your dormitory room and bid farewell to your family, you must first receive a tour to familiarize yourself with the campus."

"Startastic," said Archer, rolling his eyes.

Gran poked him in the shoulder. "Don't be rude, young man," she said.

"Sorry, Gran," he said sheepishly.

Sage glanced around. More Bot-Bot guides had appeared and were taking other new students and their families on their tours, setting off in all directions. She turned back to her family, then did a double take. Wait—someone was missing.

"Where's Mom?" she asked.

"She's right he—well, she *was* right here," said her father, looking around. "Oh, don't worry, we'll find her. You know how she's always wandering off."

Sage did know. Her mother was a very busy—and curious—woman. She was often sent on trips to distant locations to fact-find and to give talks about her specialty, interstellar positive wish energy. All Sage knew was that it took her mom away from the family frequently. That was why Gran had come to live with them when the twins were born.

"If you will follow me, we will begin our tour in the Star Quad, the heart of our state-of-the-art Starling Academy campus," announced MO-J4. He led them onto a moving walkway, which brought them to a lush green lawn. "Note the grass, perfect for relaxing or picnicking," the guide pointed out. "Here you can see the dancing fountain, the shifting hedge maze, and the band shell, where concerts are held."

"Impressive," said Sage's father, nodding.

Sage spotted a girl with an off-the-shoulder gold tunic and a halo of golden curls around her face standing on the band shell stage. She was singing and practicing some dance moves, apparently putting on her own private concert. Several students were lounging on the edge of the splashing fountain, which was tiled in a mosaic of pleasing shades of blue.

"And over here you will find the hedge maze," said MO-J4.

Sage and her family turned their attention to a tall wall of neatly trimmed greenery with an entrance cut into the side. Her little brothers' eyes lit up, and they took off toward it, disappearing into the maze without a backward glance.

"Boys!" called Gran. "We're still on the tour! Come back!"

"They'll be fine," MO-J4 assured her. "The constantly shifting paths of the hedge maze will keep them occupied for quite a while, and there are guides to help visitors find their way out if necessary." MO-J4 zoomed down to Sage's ear level and said, "Students, however, must discover the secrets of the maze all by themselves."

"No problem," said Sage in a tone more confident than she felt. She looked around. Where *was* her mother? It was just like her to disappear when Sage wanted her around. This was a big deal. Having her whole family— even her annoying little brothers—nearby would have been nice. But no, everyone seemed to want to do their own thing. Except Gran and Dad, of course.

MO-J4 next took them to the Illumination Library, a circular room crammed from floor to ceiling with thousands of tiny holo-books. Down the center of the room ran tables glowing with soft light, surrounded by lounge readers with built-in lamps. There was a padded window seat with fluffy pillows in front of each of the large windows.

Gran was impressed. "You should spend most of your time here when you're not in class," she said to her granddaughter with a nod. Sage tried not to smile as the old woman then checked out a lounge chair, which immediately adjusted to her height, weight, and preferred reading position.

Gran was less interested in the Lightning Lounge, which was housed in the same building. Sage, however, was enthralled by what she saw. It was where students went during their downtime to socialize and relax.

The lounge's main floor was split between the snack area, which was stocked with every treat and beverage the students could desire, and the sitting area, which was brightly colored and filled with floor pillows, low tables, fireplaces, fluffy rugs, soft, sumptuous chairs, and couches grouped perfectly for getting together with friends.

Downstairs was a party room big enough for dances with other schools, which were held several times a year. Next they went upstairs to cozy relaxation rooms, which sensed your mood as soon as you walked in and chose appropriate music and changed the lighting accordingly.

"Press that button on the wall to your right, Miss Sage," said MO-J4.

Sage obliged and then jumped as the ceiling high

above their heads began to roll back. "A retractable roof for stargazing," said MO-J4. "All the seats recline fully for optimal viewing comfort."

Sage smiled. They really had thought of everything to help students relax and enjoy themselves during their downtime. MO-J4 next brought them to the Celestial Café, the dining hall where students' meals were served. The view from the wall of windows was holo-card worth—the violet-hued Luminous Lake and the stunning Crystal Mountains. Sage stared at the shiny peaks. She had been dying to explore the Crystal Mountains ever since she had received a crystal for her Bright Day. Sage's dad shook his head. "Look at all this!" he said, taking in the warm lighting, the softly playing music, the table set with finery, and the Bot-Bot waiters at the students' beck and call. "When I was in school we had to bring our own lunch!"

"We must take good care of our students, sir," said MO-J4. "They need to be well fed so they can concentrate on their studies!"

They next went to Halo Hall, the largest building on campus, where all the classes were held. "Connected to this building is a tower with the famous Wishworld Surveillance Deck, accessible only to students, faculty, and graduates," MO-J4 explained.

Sage got a thrill of excitement as they peered into a neat classroom, comfortable and inviting. MO-J4 lingered in the Cybernetics Lab, a gleaming room filled with cyber-building equipment. "My home," he explained with a hint of pride in his voice.

"And then we'll go straight out these doors to the balcony, where we can get a stunning view of the fruit orchards to the north and south and of course the incomparable Crystal Mountains and Luminous Lake to the west." Everyone stepped outside and took in the view, nodding appreciatively. It was a truly breathtaking sight.

"Lovely, simply lovely," Gran murmured.

Sage's father put his hand on his daughter's shoulder. "I can't believe this is really happening," he said. "Our little Sage is about to start Starling Academy."

Sage was about to groan, "Dad, you're embarrassing me," but she held it in. Her father's eyes were shiny, and the last thing she wanted was for him to start crying. Plus he was right. This was momentous. She just didn't feel like talking about it.

"In the middle of the lake are the Serenity Gardens, accessible only by boat; and of course you can see Stellar Falls in the distance," MO-J4 noted.

"On the other side of the lake is our brother school,

Star Preparatory. Perhaps your little brothers will attend that school someday."

"Perhaps," muttered Gran before Sage could respond. The thought of her wild little brothers being studious enough to attend the prestigious school seemed like hydrongs of staryears away to Sage.

After showing them the gigantic practice Wish-House and the faculty residences—freestanding homes, each with a small backyard and garden—MO-J4 said, "Next we will move on to the Radiant Recreation Center. This is our last stop before we go to your dormitory. The recreation center is a state-of-the-art building with equipment available for every interest and sport we play on Starland. It is where our champion E-ball team, the Glowin' Glions, play every—"

Sage couldn't take the suspense any longer. "Can I go to my room now, please?" she asked. She was dying to see her room and, more important, meet her roommate.

"Sage," said Gran. "Your manners!"

MO-J4 paused again to see if the change of plan fit in with his program. "Affirmative," he concluded. Sage and her family were led past the round, gleaming rec center, along a pathway to a large white building. They stopped in front of the steps that led up to the entrance.

"There are two dormitories on campus: this is the Little Dipper Dorm, for first- and second-year students, and nearby is the Big Dipper Dorm, for third- and fourth-year students. Rooms are completely furnished for the students, with all the comforts of home, and roommates are carefully chosen to both complement and challenge each other."

Complement and *challenge*, thought Sage. *Interesting.*

Sage's father spoke up. "Sage was told not to bring anything but the clothes on her back," he said, a bit anxiously. "Are you sure she'll have everything she needs?"

"I guarantee it," said MO-J4. "Don't worry. You'll soon see what I mean."

"All right, then," said Sage's father.

"This is where I say good-bye," said MO-J4. "Once you step through the doors, hop right onto the Cosmic Transporter, which will take you directly to your room. It was a pleasure to meet you, Miss Sage. I hope we'll meet again. I will send your brothers to you. Good luck, and don't forget to count your lucky stars."

"Star salutations!" Gran and Sage's father called.

"Star salutations," Sage repeated. But MO-J4 was already gone, floating off to find her brothers.

"You should start reading it right away," Sage's

grandmother said once they had gone inside and were standing on the Cosmic Transporter, a moving sidewalk that looped throughout the entire dormitory.

"Reading what?" Sage asked.

"The Student Manual," said Gran exasperatedly.

"Oh, right," said Sage, fishing around in her pocket until she located the holo-book. She pressed a button and the manual was projected into the air in front of her. "'Welcome to Starling Academy,'" she read aloud. "'Now that you have explored the campus and are settling in, keep one extremely important thought in mind: the future of Starland depends on you.

"'As every Starling knows, the positive energy that comes from the Wishlings who live on Wishworld is our most precious natural resource. We rely on it to power our Starcars, illuminate our lights, and, in short, provide Starland with the energy it requires to function every starday.

"'You are tasked with learning how to help make Wishers' wishes come true so you can become members of the next generation of Wish-Granters. That way, the Wishers will keep making these crucial wishes, and life, for Starlings and Wishlings alike, will continue as we all know it.

"'As a student at Starling Academy, you will receive extensive, rigorous training in wish identification, wish fulfillment, wish energy capture, wishful thinking, wish probability and statistics, plus art, music, dance, and a variety of sports. . . .'"

Sage's voice trailed off. "Blah, blah, blah, blah, blah," she concluded, shutting down the holo-book with a flick of her wrist. She rolled her eyes. "No pressure or anything!" she said.

Gran laughed, but then her wrinkled face grew serious. "Sage," she scolded, "you need to pay attention. There could be some important information in that manual. It might even be on an examination!"

"What examination?" Sage asked teasingly. Her grandmother was so old-fashioned sometimes.

"An *important* examination," Gran insisted.

Sage leaned against the railing of the Cosmic Transporter. As they passed open doorways, she peeked into several of the rooms. There were girls crying as they said good-bye to their families, and others who waved merrily as their parents departed. That all made Sage even more impatient. She simply couldn't wait to see her room and meet her roommate. Finally, the transporter began to slow down. Sage straightened up as she and her family were deposited right in front of a door-way—room 261. They all stood there for a moment in silence.

They hesitated in front of the door. Suddenly, Helio and Archer came running down the Cosmic Transporter, nearly knocking into a student and her parents, who stared angrily at the boys. They jumped off the mover and dramatically rolled on the floor before coming to a stop. They bounced to their feet, not even out of breath.

"This place is pretty starmendous!" Helio shouted. "Did you see the boathouse?"

"I guess this is it," said Sage, feeling an unfamiliar fluttering in her stomach. "I . . . I think I'm a little nervous!" she admitted. Gran gave her a quizzical look. Her dad raised his eyebrows and gave her shoulder a quick squeeze.

At the same time, Archer—just as impatient as she was—reached up and slapped the hand scanner in the middle of the door.

There was a red flash and an irritating buzzing noise.

"Access denied," the Bot-Bot voice said sternly.

"Out of my way," said Sage, ruffling her brother's hair as she pushed past to show him she really wasn't mad, just pretending. She placed her hand on the scanner. "Welcome, Sage," the Bot-Bot voice said pleasantly as the scanner glowed a bright blue. They were in the right place.

The door slid open, and there stood Sage's mother.

"There you are!" she exclaimed, as though they had been the ones who had wandered off.

"How did you get in?" Sage's brother demanded.

"Oh, Sage's roommate was here," explained Indirra.

"Where is she?" Sage asked excitedly.

"She stepped out for a starmin," her mother replied.

"Where did you go, anyw . . ." Sage started. But then her eyes took in the dorm room furnishings and her voice trailed off. She stared around in disbelief. Now she understood why she had been told to come to Starling Academy empty-handed. The room was amazing. They had decorated it just the way Sage had hoped. They had asked so many questions on the school application, but this far exceeded any expectations she'd had. It reflected her personality and her love of lavender to perfection. It even had holo-powered windows so Sage could control the view!

"They've thought of everything," said her mother.

The room was circular, Sage's favorite shape, and she had a round bed and what looked like an extraordinarily comfortable round chair. Two softly glowing plants stood at either side of the bed—the perfect nightlights, in her opinion. A glimmering chandelier hung from the ceiling.

Her father blinked. "Unbelievable," he said.

Her roommate's side was pretty, too, with a star-shaped rug, a glowing staircase that led to a bed that looked a little like a very large cradle to Sage, and a single gigantic picture window with a window seat covered in sumptuous pillows.

Sage's father immediately sat on Sage's bed. "Comfy," he said.

Sage gaped at the rows of bookshelves that lined her roommate's walls. "Look at those holo-books," she marveled. "You think my roommate is a librarian or something?"

Her brothers laughed.

"Um, hello," said a small voice. Everyone turned to the open doorway, where a baby-faced girl with pale skin, big round glasses, and pinkish-white hair done up in perky little pigtail buns stood. It looked like she was trying to decide whether to step inside or run away. Despite the girl's embarrassment, Sage noticed that the girl's lashes were so thick and dark that they almost looked fake. She was wearing a light, loose shirt with spaghetti straps, shorts, swirly leggings, and pale pink ballet slippers, which laced up her legs. She was so small and neat-looking that she made Sage, who was tall and lean, feel like she was all gangly arms and legs. The girl seemed to make a decision, and she walked up to Sage uncertainly. "I'm Cassie," she said softly.

Sage gulped and smiled at her roommate. "Sorry!" she said. "It's just that you have so many books."

Gran elbowed her in the side. "And, um, I'm sure they're all very interesting!" Sage said. Impulsively, she lunged forward to hug her new roommate. Startled, the girl took a step back. She lost her balance and knocked into a pile of holo-books which sat on a table. The two girls bent down to pick them up at the same time and cracked heads. Sage rubbed her sore head and gulped again. What a way to make a first impression!

Her brothers burst out laughing. "Startastic, Sage!" Helio cried.

Sage glared at them, then turned toward her new roommate. "Sorry about that," she said. She had already apologized two times in as many starmins. That had to be some sort of new roommate record! "Um, pleased to meet you. I'm Sage and this is my family." She made a sweeping gesture. "You already met my mother. The man lying down is my father, Leonard. This is my grandmother. You can call her Gran. And the two little boys who just disappeared under your bed are my twin brothers, Helio and Archer."

Cassie looked mildly surprised at that bit of news. She stood up, adjusted her glasses, and gave Sage a tight smile—more like a grimace, actually.

"So no offense at the librarian comment?" asked Sage. "I was just trying to be funny. Just ignore it. I didn't mean any harm. The room looks great. Very homey. Actually, I love libraries. And librarians. I mean, who doesn't?" she said all in a rush.

Cassie shrugged. "No offense taken."

Sage could tell that maybe a tiny bit had been taken. But she was certain it was nothing she couldn't fix.

After taking a quick peek under her bed, Cassie began to rummage through her already jumbled drawers. Sage's father got up from her bed and stared out the window, lost in thought. Gran took one look at the slightly rumpled bed and, without warning, stripped off the linens and began remaking it. Gran certainly liked to keep busy! Sage wandered around the room, taking it all in. She stopped at the nearest closet and slid the door open.

"No!" Cassie shouted. She darted across the room,

reached past Sage, and slammed the door shut. "That's *my* closet!" She spun around, her cheeks flushed. She took a deep breath to collect herself. "I mean, um, *that* is your closet," she said more calmly, pointing across the room. Puzzled, everyone stared at her for a moment.

Note, thought Sage, *roommate is very private about her clothes.* She wouldn't be making that mistake again.

Gran fluffed Sage's pillow, then reached over to pick up a small handheld device that was sitting on Sage's desk. "What's this?" she asked.

"Got me," said Sage.

"That's a Star-Zap," Cassie explained. "We all get one. We have to keep it with us at all times, because that's how the school corresponds with us." She then gave Sage a quizzical look. "It's discussed in great detail in the Student Manual."

Gran tsk-tsked at Sage, who shrugged.

"Can we go home now?" Archer whined as he crawled out from under Cassie's bed.

Sage's mom gave a brisk nod. "Time to go home," she said. Sage's dad turned to Sage slowly. "I guess . . . it's time to leave," he said reluctantly.

"Look what I found!" cried Helio, rolling out from underneath Cassie's bed, holding a small bag of pellets.

"These look like Green Globules!" Sage gawked. They *did* look remarkably similar to the food her brothers fed their pet glowfur. (It also loved to eat flowers late at night.)

Cassie's eyes widened in alarm. "Oh, no!" she cried. "Um . . . that's actually a special snack I brought from home." And before everyone's astonished eyes, she selected a pellet and popped it into her mouth. "*Mmmm*, delicious," she mumbled. But her face told a different story.

Well, that was weird, Sage thought. Her family just stared at Cassie.

"That really did look like a Green Globule," Archer said, shaking his head. "Disgusting." He knew that quite well, Sage remembered, because he had once eaten one himself on a dare from his twin.

"Well, thanks for everything," Sage said brightly to her family. "Bye!" She hated long, drawn-out farewells. When Sage had said good-bye to her friends back home, she had made it short and sweet, too. Sure, she was sad. But there was no sense in making something painful even harder than it needed to be.

Her father squeezed her tight. "I'm so proud of you, Toodles," he whispered into her ear, using her embarrassing family nickname. He opened his mouth as if he was going to say something else, then just settled for another hug.

That gave Sage an uncomfortable lump in her throat. She squirmed out of his grasp. "Good-bye, Dad," she said.

Gran hated good-byes, too. "See ya around, kid," she said with a wink.

At their father's urging, the twins each gave Sage a hug, as well, but each one was so brief that it was as if she had a contagious illness they were afraid of contracting. Still, Sage knew they would miss her, if only because she helped them with their homework and would, if asked nicely, eat all their garble greens for them so they could get dessert.

Sage's mom put her hands on Sage's shoulders and gave her a quick, firm embrace. She stepped back and looked deep into Sage's violet eyes. "Make me proud, my dear," she said. Then she leaned forward and whispered in her ear, "You're startacular, and don't you forget it."

Sage snapped back her head to stare at her mother. "Th-thanks, Mom," she stammered. Her mom's compliments were rare, so when she gave one, you knew she meant it. When Sage was younger, she used to be jealous of kids whose mothers smothered them with accolades. "You're the brightest star in the galaxy" or "You glimmer like a supernova." But as she got older, she grew to appreciate her mother's measured but heartfelt words of praise. It felt like Sage had earned them.

Studies had never been easy for her, and she sometimes felt like she was disappointing her mom. Sage had had to work hard for every I (which stood for Illuminated, the top grade a student could receive) she was awarded. So her mother's words really meant a lot.

Indirra touched her daughter's cheek, then joined the rest of the family in the hallway. After a moment, Sage slid the door closed behind them.

The two girls stared at each other for a moment.

Sage flopped down on the bed Gran had remade so neatly, and clutched her pillow to her chest. "So, tell me everything about you," she said to Cassie. "Don't leave anything out!"

Cassie looked around the room wildly, positively panicked. "Um . . . I . . ."

Just then their Star-Zaps beeped. They both looked down at their display screens: REPORT TO THE STAR QUAD IN TWENTY STARMINS FOR THE START OF THE WELCOME PROCESSION.

"Welcome procession?" said Sage.

Cassie gave her a look.

"It's in the Student Manual?" Sage guessed.

"It's in the Student Manual," Cassie answered.

Sage considered that. "Want to fill me in?" she asked.

"Well, it's a Starling Academy tradition going back hydrongs of staryears. New students parade around the campus as the faculty and upperclassmen welcome them. Everyone wears fancy clothes and it's said to be really special. Supposedly, we're about to receive the most amazing outfits we've ever seen," said Cassie.

As if on command, there was a knock at the door. When they opened it, a Bot-Bot deliverer was hovering in the hallway, holding aloft two remarkable outfits—one lavender, one white.

"Wow," said Sage, grabbing the dresses. "Star salutations." She brought them inside and handed the white one to Cassie.

"It's startacular," said Cassie softly, touching the shiny material.

Sage nodded. "It's like they took the best parts of all my favorite dresses and made one perfect outfit."

"Once we're dressed, we'll head to the quad. Lady Stella will greet us and the procession will begin," Cassie said.

Sage looked at her beautiful dress, her eyes shining. She grinned. Things were finally starting to happen. It was about time!

CHAPTER
2

"**How do I look?**" Cassie asked shyly. Sage took one last look in the mirror and turned to face her roommate.

"Beautiful," she told her. Cassie was wearing a sheer white dress embroidered with a sprinkling of silvery stardust. The waist was cinched with a wide silver sash tied in the back in a big bow. Underneath she wore a simple glimmering silver slip. On her head was a wide headband of glowing moons and stars. Glitter slippers completed the ensemble.

"You look lovely, too," Cassie told Sage.

"Star salutations," replied Sage. She felt magical. Although her usual style of dress was simple and comfortable, she absolutely loved the floor-length dress and its layers upon ruffled layers of the softest lavender fabric. She admired the sheer bell sleeves and smoothed her braids, threaded with the tiniest twinkling lights she had ever seen.

The two girls headed to the Star Quad. Before she knew it, Sage was separated from Cassie, swept away in a sea of students, all smiling and laughing. It seemed as if everyone, even the girls who had had the hardest time saying good-bye to their families, was delighted to be at Starling Academy and thrilled to be in her fancy best. There were girls in ball gowns and dresses with long trains, and others with huge ruffles that spilled down their fronts. They wore jeweled tiaras, fluffy boas, and hats of all shapes and sizes: a fascinator with flowers, a towering bright pink top hat with a face-obscuring net.

Sage felt like she was part of a big, happy, festive party as they all slowly made their way to the Star Quad. A girl with long, shiny hair the same shade of pink as cotton candy stumbled on her long train and momentarily clutched Sage's arm for support. "Isn't this exciting?" she cried, looping her pink skirt over her arm. Sage nodded. It was actually the very definition of exciting, in her opinion. Finally, everyone was gathered in the Star Quad. A tall, regal-looking woman stepped onto the stage. She had sparkling olive skin and bright red lips and wore a long, flowing midnight-blue gown with enormous sleeves that shimmered like the heavens at night. A single golden star sat in the middle of her forehead. But it was her headdress that really took Sage's breath away—a galaxy of stars clustered around her head, neck, and shoulders, spinning and glittering. A hush fell over the crowd.

"I am Lady Stella," she said, although she needed no introduction. She was so famous as headmistress of the most prestigious school in all of Starland that her name was often in the holo-papers and her face on the news. Some truly obsessed girls even dressed up like Lady Stella on Light Giving Day—the holiday celebrating the first starday of the Time of New Beginnings, when Starling children dressed up in costumes and went door-to-door distributing newly bloomed flowers.

Every student in the room had gone through the same rigorous process in the hope of attending Starling Academy: application forms, essays, testing, recommendations. Only a small percentage of those who applied were granted an interview with the headmistress. And an even smaller percentage of girls was accepted. Starling Academy had a 100 percent attendance rate: every student who was admitted chose to enroll. Every year.

Lady Stella continued. "Welcome to Starling Academy and the student procession. It is a time-honored tradition for our newest students to dress in their finest clothes and walk through the campus to be received by students and faculty. We welcome you to the Starling Academy community and congratulate you on your acceptance. We thank you for joining us in the pursuit of knowledge and positive wish energy." She raised her arms. "Let the procession begin!"

A marching band began to play, and the girls started the procession. Teachers and the second-, third-, and fourth-year students, also dressed in their finest clothes, lined up along the walkways and leaned down from windows and balconies to cheer. Sage spotted a student, dressed almost entirely in black with accents of hot pink, standing apart from the others.

Iridescent bubbles filled the air, releasing the sweet scent of glimmerberries as they popped. There was something so special, so amazing about being a part of the experience. When the new students passed the Big Dipper Dorm, girls standing on the balcony cheered, showering them with flower petals that changed color as they floated down and disappeared when they hit the ground.

WELCOME NEW STUDENTS appeared in the sky in

glittering script. Sage grinned as she took in the dizzying beauty of the scene. *I will remember this forever,* she thought.

After the procession, the students were led into the auditorium, where Sage settled into a plush seat. *Very comfy,* she thought as she softly bounced up and down.

Just then she remembered something: *Hey, where's Cassie?* Sage craned her neck and looked around the room. She spotted her roommate several rows behind her, wearing a serious expression, her arms folded tightly across her chest. Sage gave Cassie a huge wave and pointed to the empty seat next to her. But the seat was immediately filled by a girl with pale blue hair with bangs and a fringed dress of the same exact color.

"Sorry," said Sage pleasantly, "but this seat is taken."

"Yeah," said the girl, an unpleasant smile on her face. "By me."

Sage was fuming, but she decided to let it go. She turned back to Cassie and shrugged.

Everyone in the audience spoke in hushed voices and sat up very straight, well aware of the significance of that starday. Some of the girls were already whispering together as if they had been friends forever. Sage felt a stab of excitement. It was possible that somewhere in that room was her future best friend. But then she thought her future biggest enemy could be there, too.

The crowd burst into thunderous applause as Lady Stella stepped onto the stage. "Welcome to Starling Academy," Lady Stella began. "I hope you enjoyed the welcome procession. You are an extremely exceptional group of students. Almost every girl on our star who has reached the Age of Fulfillment applies for a spot in Starling Academy. You've all worked very hard to get here and we are happy to have you."

Sage felt a flush of pride. Simply sitting there in the auditorium was already an accomplishment. "And now, you are about to begin the most important work of your lives." Lady Stella paused.

"As we all know, you are all here to begin your training to become Wish-Granters. Once your education is complete, you will be on your way to collecting the precious wish energy that keeps Starland operating." She paused and nodded. "And as you also know, Wishlings make many wishes," she continued. "As they are about to blow out their birthday candles." Sage sniffed appreciatively as the smell of chocolate cake filled the room. "On a shooting star streaking across the sky," Lady Stella added. The lights went out and the ceiling twinkled with starlight, a bright flash splitting the sky. She continued. "As they blow on a dandelion gone to seed." Sage reached up to touch one of the small white tufts that appeared and danced around the room. "As they toss a coin into a fountain." Students squealed as they were sprinkled with cool water droplets. "And I don't need to tell you that the wishes of Wishling children, in particular, are the purest and produce the greatest amount of energy."

The headmistress nodded and continued. "As everyone knows, when a wish is made, it turns into a glowing Wish Orb, invisible to the Wisher's eyes. The wish rapidly flies through the heavens to Starland. When the Wish Orb arrives, it is collected by a Wish Catcher, who determines whether it is a good wish, a bad wish, or an impossible wish.

"The Good Wish Orbs sprout pretty sparkly stems and are brought to the Wish-House where they are tended to and observed by trained Wish-Watchers. It can take anywhere from a few starmins to a few staryears for a wish to be ready to be granted. That is when it emits the most wonderful, magical glow. It is the most amazing sight to see, even if a Starling has seen it a thousand times.

"Then the Wish Orb is presented to the appropriate Starling for wish fulfillment. Once a good wish is granted and the wish energy collected, the Wish Orb transforms into a unique and beautiful Wish Blossom.

"Bad Wish Orbs are another story. They sprout stems that don't sparkle and are immediately transported to a special containment center, as they are very dangerous and must not be granted.

"Impossible Wish Orbs sprouts stems that sparkle with an unbearably bright light. They are taken to a special area of the Wish-House with tinted windows to cut down on the glare they produce. They are monitored in the hopes that one day they can be turned into good wishes that are within our powers to help grant. Here at Star Academy we have a state-of-the-art practice Wish-House where you will learn to do exactly that."

Sage rolled her eyes. Every Starling toddler knew that stuff—boring! She sighed and turned around to look at Cassie. Surely she was feeling restless, too. But Cassie was completely focused on the headmistress, with the same very serious expression on her face. Unable to catch her roommate's eye, Sage looked around the room. She spotted a girl whispering to her seatmate. Her orange hair was done in a beautiful upswept style. The girl must have sensed someone's eyes on her, because she turned around, caught Sage staring, and stuck out her tongue at Sage. Sage didn't know whether to laugh or be mad. She quickly looked away. What a saucy Starling! Sage turned her attention back to the headmistress, who was still talking.

"... and so I am happy to report that this year's class is our most talented yet. Be prepared to study hard, learn a lot, and accomplish great things, and soon you will be on your way to graduating and becoming Wish-Granters," Lady Stella concluded. "Are there any questions?"

Sage raised her hand. The headmistress shaded her eyes. "Yes?" she said.

"When do we get started?" Sage asked.

Heads swiveled around and there were a couple of giggles. Sage barely noticed.

"And what is your name, my dear?" Lady Stella asked.

"Sage," she replied.

The headmistress smiled and nodded as if she had known that all along. "Before you know it, Sage," she said. "Before you know it."

Lady Stella clapped her hands together. "So, now, everyone take out your Star-Zaps. You will be meeting in small groups for your formal orientation. You will receive a message telling you where you need to go."

Sage placed her communicator on her lap and stared at the blank screen expectantly.

"I'm group one!" shouted a girl.

"Me too!" said another.

Sage looked over the shoulder of the girl sitting in front of her. The girl's screen lit up. GROUP 3, it said. Then: REPORT TO CONSTELLATION CLASSROOM 313.

Sage watched in dismay as girl after girl received her assignment and headed to her classroom, some joining up with fellow classmates and chattering excitedly. Still, her screen remained maddeningly blank.

Finally, it lit up: SD. She stared at the letters, her brow furrowed. That made no sense.

What does that mean? she wondered. The next message read REPORT TO HEADMISTRESS'S OFFICE.

Sage nodded. Headmistress's office? Now things were getting interesting!

The girl sitting next to Sage peered down at Sage's communicator from beneath her long, pale blue bangs. " 'SD'?" she said. "What does *that* stand for?" She turned to the girl next to her and elbowed her in the side before adding snidely, "I know—Super Dorky!"

Sage thought fast. "Actually, it means . . . Superbly Delightful," she countered.

The girl paused for a moment. "So Doubtful," she finally crowed, obviously pleased with herself.

Well, you are most definitely *not going to be my new best friend,* thought Sage as she stood, pushed her way past the girl, and headed down the aisle.

Sage jumped as a cold hand reached out and grabbed her elbow. She spun around, ready for another confrontation. But it was Cassie, biting her lip and looking worried. "Sage?" she said. "I just got a weird message, and I'm not sure what to think."

"SD?" asked Sage.

Cassie's face brightened. "Yes, you too?" she asked.

"Me too," replied Sage with a nod.

"Superstar!" Cassie said, looking very relieved.

"I think it must be something good," mused Sage.

Cassie blinked. "I . . . I hope so," she said. "But I'm a little worried. What if we're in trouble or something?"

Sage laughed. How funny. That had never even crossed her mind. "Only time will tell!" she said. She leaned down slightly to link arms with her roommate, and the two walked to the headmistress's office together. It was nice to face the unknown with someone familiar by your side. Even if you had just met her for the first time a short while earlier. Even if she ate strange snacks. And had weird closet issues. Even then.

CHAPTER
3

Sage counted again. Twelve. Including herself, there were twelve girls seated at the round silver table in the headmistress's enormous office. Each seat had a holo–place card in front of it. Sage was sitting between Tessa, a girl with bright green curls who seemed really kind, and Adora, whose eyes were an amazing shade of light blue. Everyone was dressed in their finery, and it looked like they were all sitting down to a fancy dinner party—minus the place settings and the food, of course. Sage was across from a girl in a black mask with pink sequins. Sage frowned as she took in the girl's magenta eyes and fuchsia hair. She wore a puffy layered skirt and a short-sleeved rhinestone-trimmed jacket with an enormous ruffled collar over a hot-pink-and-black-striped blouse. She also had on black lace gloves. She was very striking. Wasn't she the same girl Sage had spotted standing on the balcony during the procession? And didn't that mean she was an upperclassman? What was she doing at new student orientation? It was all very confusing.

Sage then looked curiously at the others around the table, matching each face with the name on the place card. Adora, Tessa, Gemma (who was chatting away; Sage recognized her as the girl who had stuck out her tongue in the auditorium), Vega, Leona (who had been singing and dancing on the quad), Clover, Libby (the girl in pink who had tripped on her train during the procession), Piper, Astra, Cassie, and Scarlet (the masked upperclassman). Sage noticed that Vega looked a bit worried and Piper seemed lost in thought, twirling a piece of her seafoam-green hair around her finger. Libby was studying everyone intently.

Astra, who somehow managed to make her bright red gown look sporty, was attempting to have a friendly chat with Cassie, who was shooting glances around the room, apparently unable to concentrate on small talk. Sage herself felt like she was going to jump out of her skin if she didn't find out what was going on. Immediately.

Then the office door slid open and Lady Stella glided inside. She looked at the girls assembled around the table, carefully studying each one. Sage gazed right back at her. Lady Stella was even lovelier up close. Her sparkling olive skin was smooth and flawless, and her eyes danced in the light from her glimmering headpiece.

Sage watched as the headmistress closed her eyes for a moment, as if to collect her thoughts. Then she said something truly incredible.

"You twelve girls are about to make Starling history," she pronounced solemnly.

There were several gasps. "Moons and stars!" Cassie cried, looking apprehensive. Sage, on the other hand, felt elated. This was good. Very good.

"What in the stars are you talking about?" cried Gemma.

"Gemma!" scolded Tessa. "Don't be rude!"

Sage stared at the two girls. Did they know each other?

"But I really want to know!" Gemma exclaimed. "I mean, you can't just say something like that and leave us hanging! I mean, I'm really . . ."

Tessa leaned forward and placed her hand over Gemma's mouth.

Everyone stared. *That* seemed pretty inappropriate.

Lady Stella laughed at their shocked faces. "Gemma and Tessa are sisters," she told everyone.

"Okay, back to business. Let me explain what I mean. We have always known that the greatest amount of positive energy is generated by granting the wishes of young Wishlings. Traditionally, this has been done only by Starling adults who have graduated from a wish-granting academy. But I have a theory that if the wishes of young Wishlings were to be granted by young Starlings, this special combination would produce an even greater amount of positive wish energy. My plan is for Starling Academy students to go down to Wishworld for the first time in history and test this theory."

A stunned silence filled the room.

"It makes perfect sense," she said. "Young Starlings could attend school, join teams and clubs, and blend in seamlessly with young Wishlings."

Sage looked down at the table, barely holding back a small smile. Starling Academy students traveling to Wishworld and granting wishes? Amazing! She was pretty sure she knew what was coming next, and she held her breath in anticipation.

"And who are these lucky students? All of you, of course! Twelve talented girls who are as unique as those they are going to help. Four third years—Scarlet, Leona, Tessa, and Adora. Four second years—Piper, Vega, Clover, and Astra. And four first years—Sage, Cassie, Libby, and Gemma."

The twelve girls stared at Lady Stella in silence as the weight of her words sank in.

Cassie was the first to speak. She looked stricken. "I don't get it!" she cried. "Why me? Why us?"

Lady Stella smiled a secret smile. "It will all be revealed in due time," she said.

The room began to buzz with excited chatter. Sage could see why Cassie might be apprehensive—Starlings had to train for four years before they were allowed to travel down to Wishworld to grant wishes! But to Sage, this was nothing but a thrilling, unexpected gift.

Lady Stella held up a hand for silence, and everyone immediately stopped talking.

"If our calculations are correct, the amount of positive energy you collect could be up to a thousand times greater than usual."

The headmistress had a serious look on her face. "There is just one thing you must know: this is highly controversial and must remain a secret. To the rest of the school, you are students, just like them. You will attend classes with your fellow classmates. You will join teams and participate in clubs. To the rest of Starling Academy, you will be no different from any other student."

She smiled. "Except for one small thing: during the last period of each starday, you will report to a specially built soundproof classroom for a class only for you. In order to divert attention away from our secret plans, the rest of the school will think you are part of a monitored study group."

"You can't possibly mean us, too!" exclaimed Leona, indicating herself and the other seven older girls.

"I mean every one of you," Lady Stella answered.

"Wait a starmin," said Vega, clearly dismayed. "You mean no one will know that we're on this special mission? That they will think we need extra help?"

"This is not about personal glory," Lady Stella said sternly. "If you don't want to be a part of Starling history, you can turn down your spot. Another student will certainly jump at the opportunity."

Lady Stella extended her arms dramatically. "So," she said. "Are you all in?"

"Yes!" shouted Sage right away.

Astra gave her a dirty look. Clearly she had wanted to be the first to speak. "Yes," she said.

All around the table, the girls accepted the challenge. Some were more emphatic in their response than others.

When it was finally Cassie's turn, she paused for what felt like an eternity before stealing a glance at Sage, who nodded at her encouragingly. "Yes," she whispered.

"Starmendous!" said Lady Stella. She then pointed to the middle of the table, where a large pile of glittery golden boxes in all shapes and sizes sat. Sage blinked. She was fairly certain the center of the table had been empty just a moment ago. From the looks on the other girls' faces, they thought the same thing.

The headmistress picked up a small square box. "Clover," she announced. "Please stand up." She opened the box to reveal a jeweled purple barrette. She clipped it into Clover's hair, where it winked in the light.

"This is your Wish Pendant," Lady Stella explained to Clover. She looked around the room. "You will each receive your own. As you all know, students usually receive these upon graduating, but you are getting them now. You may take it off at night, but you should wear it every day. Wish Pendants are of utmost importance on Wish Missions. They will glow when you make initial contact with your Wisher. They will collect the wish energy when the wish is granted. And, since you are Star Darlings, your Wish Pendants will hold extra special powers," she explained mysteriously. "This will be revealed as your education progresses."

Lady Stella continued to hand out the boxes. A watch for Adora. Bracelets for Piper. Sporty Astra looked quite pleased with her wristband. Tessa admired her brooch. Gemma was presented with earrings. Libby got a necklace of tiny clustered stars, and Scarlet received star-shaped buckles for her boots. Leona fastened a thick cuff on her arm. Cassie received a pair of very cool-looking star-shaped glasses, which she seemed delighted with, despite herself. Vega accepted her belt buckle solemnly.

Lady Stella slipped a sparkling gold star pendant around Sage's neck. It hung from a long lavender rope accented with tiny stars. It was beautiful to look at, and she could somehow sense that it had great powers. She found herself trembling as she admired it.

There was a rap at the door. Lady Stella inclined her head and the door slid open. A short, stocky woman with purple hair stood uncomfortably in the doorway. "Allow me to introduce Lady Cordial, our head of admissions," Lady Stella said.

"Hello, s-s-s-students," Lady Cordial said in a low voice.

"Lady Cordial is our admissions director and is instrumental in helping select each incoming class. I have decided to share your secret mission with her. She, a Wish-Watcher who will notify us when our wishes are ready to be granted, and a few of your professors will be the only Starling Academy members who know of your mission. Please introduce yourselves to her." So one by one, the girls stood up and said their names, doing the traditional Starling bow. Lady Cordial clasped her hands together after each bow, the Starling way.

"S-s-s-star s-s-s-salutations, girls," she said when they were done.

"Star salutations, Lady Cordial," the girls chorused.

"Now go to the Celestial Café, have a nice dinner, and get a good night's sleep. Your classes begin first thing tomorrow morning. Your schedules have already been sent to your communicators," Lady Stella told them.

Sage felt a shiver of excitement run down her spine as she stood up from the table. Cassie, her eyes large behind her glasses and her face even paler than usual, made a beeline for Sage. "I don't know about this, Sage. What have we gotten ourselves into?"

Sage patted her roommate's arm reassuringly. *What have we gotten ourselves into?* she thought. *Just the most amazingly startastic thing ever!* Cassie turned and headed out the door. Sage followed her and paused to tap her elbows together three times as inconspicuously as she could.

"Three times for good luck," someone said.

Startled, Sage turned around to find the headmistress smiling down at her. "You are eager to begin," Lady Stella said. "I like that!" She turned to walk away.

"Lady Stella!" Sage called.

"Yes?" said the headmistress.

"What does SD stand for, anyway?" Sage asked.

Lady Stella nodded. "I was wondering when someone was going to ask. You will be known—in private only, of course—as the Star Darlings."

Sage smiled. "Star Darlings," she whispered to herself. It was a good name. She liked it. A lot.

CHAPTER
4

"Let me see your schedule," said Sage that evening, standing in the middle of the room in a lavender nightgown. She had cleaned her teeth with her brand-new toothlight and taken a sparkle shower to keep her skin shiny and glittery, and she was almost ready for bed. Cassie accessed her holo-schedule, and Sage synced hers up with a flick of her wrist. Their one class in common—Lighterature, fifth period—lit up.

As first years, they had all introductory classes. Sage had Wishers 101 first period, Intro to Wish Identification second, and Intro to Wishful Thinking third. After lunch she had Astral Accounting, Lighterature, Intro to Wish Fulfillment, and The Golden Days. On Shinedays she had P.E.—Physical Energy—and every Lunaday she had Aspirational Art. And, as Lady Stella had told them, the last-period class of each starday was labeled Study Group.

"Well, we'll have Lighterature and our SD classes together—better than nothing," said Cassie as she crawled into bed and pulled up her patchwork quilt to her chin. "So do you think it's going to be hard to be in classes with everyone else? We have this huge secret we have to keep from basically everybody."

Sage fluffed her pillow. "It's not going to be easy," she agreed. But she couldn't help grinning. "But it's just so exciting! I don't even know how I am going to sleep tonight!"

"Speak for yourself," said Cassie, yawning. "Are you ready for me to shut off the lights?"

"Sure," said Sage. She watched with amusement as Cassie squinched up her face, concentrating on dimming the lights. The girl was having so much trouble that Sage secretly gave her a little help.

"There," said Cassie. "I'm getting much better at my energy manipulation!"

Sage smiled and pulled the covers over her head. She anticipated tossing and turning, but she was out in moments. It had been a draining starday.

Sage was in the Illumination Library, doing some research. She wasn't making a peep. But for some reason, the librarian was telling her to be quiet. "*Shhhhhhh!*" she hissed.

Confused, Sage looked up from her Star-Zap and gave her a "Who, me?" look.

"*Shhhhh!*" said the librarian, more loudly this time.

Sage shook her head. "But I'm not talking," she said in a loud whisper.

"*Shhhhhhh!*" the librarian said again, suddenly morphing into the tall, rude girl with the pale blue bangs from the auditorium. "Didn't you hear me say *shhhhh?*" Her eyes grew mean. "Oh, that's right, you're an SD— Sad Disappointment!"

"That's not what it stands for!" Sage yelled. "I'm a Star Darling! I'm going to travel to Wishworld right now! I'm going to collect one thousand times the wish energy of anyone else."

Everyone in the library spun around and goggled at her, their mouths open in surprise. All too late, Sage realized what she had done.

"Oops," she said, her heart sinking.

Her adversary laughed cruelly. "You told the secret. Now you can't be a Star Darling anymore," she screeched. "Too bad for you!" She put her finger to her lips: "*Shhhhhhhhhhhhhhhhhhhhhhhhhhhhhhhhhhh!*"

Sage woke with a start. The room was still dark. It was the middle of the night and she had been dreaming. But then she heard that strange shushing noise again—and it was coming from right across the room. Sage rubbed her eyes. Cassie, whispering and giggling, was bathed in a golden glow. Was it Sage's imagination, or did she hear a funny little musical buzzing sound? It was quite lovely, actually.

I must still be dreaming, Sage thought. And she promptly fell back asleep.

When she woke up the next morning, Cassie was sliding her closet door closed. "Hey, Cassie," said Sage, sitting up in bed. "I had the weirdest dream last night. You were giggling and there was this weird, beautiful sound. . . ."

Cassie's eyes widened behind her glasses. "Dreams can be so strange," she said quickly.

Sage frowned. It had all seemed so real. She got out of bed, opened her closet door, and pulled on a long sleeveless lavender dress, lavender tights, and gladiator sandals that laced up her legs. She looked at her reflection in the mirror. Nice: flowing and comfortable, her favorite combination.

"Ready for breakfast?" asked Cassie.

Sage's stomach rumbled. "Sounds good to me!" she said. She picked up her communicator from the desk and put it in her pocket. As she took one quick glance back over her shoulder, she thought she saw a faint glow coming from Cassie's closet. She was about to say something, but Cassie practically pushed her out of the room. By the time the door slid shut behind them with a *whoosh*, it had completely slipped Sage's mind.

They hopped on the Cosmic Transporter and joined other students as they made their way to the Celestial Café. Adora was waving to them from across the room, where she sat with her roommate, Tessa, as well as Libby and Gemma. "Nice table," said Sage, pulling out a chair and sitting down. The view of the Crystal Mountains was starmendous.

As the rest of the Star Darlings arrived for breakfast, Adora waved them over.

"I have an idea," said Astra, looking around. "Let's make this our table. A bunch of girls who graduated last year used to sit here, so now it could be ours."

Scarlet rolled her eyes, but everyone else seemed to think that was a good idea.

When Sage's breakfast arrived, she discovered that she didn't have much of an appetite. Too excited to eat,

she picked at her starcakes. She was amused that the usually anxious Cassie polished off her bowl of Sparkle-O's
(a glimmering cereal that Sage's mom would never buy,
despite her little brothers' begging and pleading) and
even asked the Bot-Bot waiter for seconds.

"Certainly, Cassie," it said, zipping off to the kitchen.
Sage sipped at her steaming mug of Zing and moved her
food around on her plate.

"So tell me where you're from, Cassie," she said to
her roommate.

"Old Prism," Cassie told her. Sage nodded. Old
Prism was a medium-sized city about an hour from campus. It was one of Starland's original settlements and was
a popular tourist destination. Sage had gone there once
on a class trip.

"Do you have any starkin?" Sage asked.

Cassie shook her head.

"Lucky!" said Sage. "So it's just you and your mom
and dad, huh?"

Cassie paused a moment, then nodded.

"What do your parents do?" Sage asked. "My mom is
a scientist and my dad works for the government. Gran
stays with us while my parents are at work."

Cassie thought for a moment. "My mom works at

the Old Prism museum and my dad is a doctor," she said softly.

"Well, I'm sorry I missed them at drop-off," Sage said. "I guess I'll meet them at Parents' Weekend. We could all go out for lunch or something. If you don't mind my crazy little brothers, that is."

Cassie stared at her bowl. "Maybe," she said.

Their Star-Zaps began to vibrate and flash. It was time for first period. The girls all stood and gave each other encouraging smiles.

"I'm off to Wishers 101," said Sage.

"Well, that sounds way better than Astral Accounting," said Cassie. "Bo-ring."

"I'll have that soon enough," said Sage. "Have fun, Cassie." The two girls left the cafeteria and headed in opposite directions, Sage walking to Constellation Classroom 113. She stepped inside the room and immediately felt the nervous excitement of all the students. The first class of the first starday at the top wish-granting school on Starland. Pretty starmendous. Sage settled into a seat, which immediately adjusted itself to her body. Ahhhh . . . comfort.

She listened carefully as the teacher began to speak. Her Star-Zap was recording everything, and when she went to bed that night, she would put on her headphones and play back the lectures from the starday so she would absorb the information as she slept. It was the most efficient way to study.

"Welcome to Wishers 101," the teacher said. An older woman with piercing blue eyes and fading purple hair, she was draped in colorful star-covered clothing and clutched a blue staff. She was hunched over and very wrinkly. "My name is Professor Elara Ursa and I am a former Wish-Granter, with the greatest number of wish missions of any Wish-Granter in Starland history," she said in a raspy voice. She was quite intimidating.

"Wishlings and Starlings look remarkably alike," the professor began. "Wishlings have a range of different skin, eye, and hair colors, just as we do. But their natural tones are not as vivid as ours. And their skin does not have our sparkling glow. But never fear. Once you have graduated and are on your way to your first Wish Mission, this will be easily adjusted by putting your hand on your Wish Pendant and repeating these words: "Star light, star bright, the first star I see tonight: I wish I may, I wish I might, have the wish I wish tonight."

Sage repeated the words to herself. Just for practice.

"There are many other differences that you must be aware of to be able to blend in seamlessly on Wishworld," the teacher cautioned. "Clothing is one. Each Star-Zap comes with an outfit changer so you can select Wishling clothing. Their clothing is made from materials found only on their planet, and they do not have access to the stain-free fibers that grow in abundance on Starland."

A girl with short bright orange hair raised her hand. Professor Elara Ursa pointed to her. "Yes, what is your name?"

"Tweela," said the girl.

"What is your question, Tweela?"

"Does that mean Wishlings actually have to wash their clothing?" Tweela asked incredulously.

Professor Elara Ursa nodded. "They do. Also, their clothing eventually wears out and often needs to be replaced."

The room buzzed. That was so very strange!

"Wishlings also have to clean their homes," Professor Elara Ursa continued. "They do not have self-cleaning houses like we do. Wishlings may spend many hours a week keeping their surroundings dirt free."

Another student raised her hand. "So does that mean they don't have vanishing garbage?"

"Sadly for them, they do not," said the professor, trying unsuccessfully to hide her disgusted expression. "None of their trash disappears. People driving giant loud trucks ride around, grab cans full of garbage, and dump it into a massive crushing machine." She closed her eyes and shook her head. "Absolutely disgusting!" she muttered under her breath, but Sage, sitting close by, heard her.

Collecting garbage? What a strange thing to do! Sage was surprised. Life on Wishworld sounded a lot more primitive than she had imagined!

A girl in red raised her hand. "What is the weather like on Wishworld? How will we know how to dress to blend in?"

"An excellent question," said Professor Elara Ursa. "Wishlings have four seasons, as we do. But they have different names. They call the Time of New Beginnings spring. The Time of Lumiere is called summer on Wishworld. They call the Time of Letting Go fall, and the Time of Shadows is known as winter. The temperatures vary widely depending on where you are, and your outfit changer will only access weather-appropriate outfits."

Interesting, thought Sage. She'd never be able to keep all that straight!

"Do they celebrate the same holidays we do?" a serious-looking girl with purple pigtails asked.

"They do not," answered Professor Elara Ursa.

"Wishlings celebrate the new year in the middle of the Time of Shadows. This is followed by a holiday celebrating love and affection, called Valentine's Day. They give each other paper cards expressing their admiration for each other and gifts shaped like the heart organ. Some of these heart shapes contain a delicacy called chocolate— and Wishlings think it's delicious, but it's really dreadful. If you ever are offered a chocolate, I highly recommend turning it down. This is followed by a holiday when many Wishlings wear green and march in parades and men in skirts play noisy instruments. There are also holidays celebrating eggs and rabbits, and one when they eat a lot and say thank you. Wishlings place large fir trees in their homes, which bloom with attractive ornaments. Then they place colorful wrapped boxes underneath."

The girls laughed. How bizarre!

"Yes, Wishlings and their holidays can be quite strange!" the professor concluded.

Sage thought that Wishling holidays sounded interesting, but she felt sorry that they didn't know anything about Starland holidays. Imagine not celebrating the Festival of Illumination, when family and friends got together to eat cocomoon fritters and set off light rockets at night. Or Starshine Day, held on the warmest starday of Lumiere, with hiking, rock climbing, games, and sing-alongs of traditional songs. Or going door-to-door with her brothers on Light Giving Day, then returning home for zoomberry cake. She couldn't imagine life without any of those special days.

Sage's head was spinning. There was so much information to take in. Life on Wishworld certainly was different! She hoped it would all be absorbed by her brain overnight, because she was having trouble concentrating at the moment.

"There is so much for you to learn about Wishling culture," said Professor Elara Ursa. "Wishworld is a complicated, very odd place." She smiled. "But don't take my word for it. As part of this class, we will routinely go to the Wishworld Surveillance Deck and do some Wishworld Wishling watching! Come, let's go right now!"

"Wishworld Wishling watching!" the girl named Tweela repeated with a laugh. "Try to say that three times fast!" And then she did. Unsuccessfully.

Sage tried it herself as she stood and joined the others filing out of the classroom, but she couldn't do it, either. She followed the group down a long hallway, to a Flash Vertical Mover that was waiting for them, its glass doors open. They stepped inside and the doors whooshed shut.

Sage's ears popped as the mover gained speed, taking them up, up, up the enormously high tower. She swallowed hard as the ground below and the buildings of Starling Academy became tinier and tinier. Luckily, she wasn't afraid of heights.

Ding! They had arrived. By neatly dodging around the other students as they exited the mover, Sage was the first to push open the glass doors and step outside onto the surveillance deck. She froze. She had never seen anything more spectacular. The sky was so clear she could see for floozels.

Stars twinkled, distant planets glowed, and every so often a white-hot shooting star streaked across the sky. She wondered if someone was on the way down to Wishworld at that very moment. Sage finally understood the true meaning of the word *breathtaking*.

"Welcome to the Wishworld Surveillance Deck," said Professor Elara Ursa. "Find yourself a telescope and start observing!" On the ledge of the deck were dozens of large telescopes. Although there were more than enough for everyone, the students bumped into each other in their excitement to get to them. Sage found a free telescope and placed her hands on its cool metal surface. She put her eye to the eyepiece and peered through.

Then she jumped back in surprise—everything was so close—before leaning forward for another look.

The telescope was so incredibly powerful that it was as if she was right there on Wishworld, not on a distant star mooniums of floozels away. She could not believe her eyes. It was so shockingly magnificent that for a star-sec she thought it might be a dream.

She saw a female Wishling walking with a small furry animal in a park. She had a sudden start as she realized just how similar Starlings and Wishlings actually looked.

"I see a Wishling animal!" she cried. The other students rushed over to take a look and marvel at how adorable it was. Sage thought it was almost as cute as her brother's pet glowfur.

"That's called a dog," said Professor Elara Ursa. "Many Wishlings keep them as pets and take them on walks several times a day." She went on to explain that many Wishworld animals did not live together as harmoniously as the plant-eating creatures of Starland, which was a lush place with an abundance of plants for the animals to eat. But there were still some similarities. Flutterfocuses were akin to Wishworld butterflies, and globerbeems a lot like Wishworld lightning bugs. Wishworld horses were the closest animal to galliopes.

And the glion was a gentle and distant cousin to the Wishworld lion.

Sage moved the telescope a tiny bit and next spotted a young male Wishling tossing an oddly shaped brown ball. She paused for a moment to watch the ball arc through the air before a second young male Wishling caught it in his hands. *They really do look a lot like Starling boys*, she thought. *Just not as sparkly, but still cute.* She next noticed a group of small Wishlings in a circle holding hands as they sang. To her surprise, they suddenly collapsed on the ground. Was something wrong? But they almost immediately jumped to their feet, laughing out loud. It was a game! It didn't look like such a fun one to her, but it certainly seemed as if they were enjoying it.

As she moved the telescope this way and that, watching Wishlings at rest, work, and play, she listened to Professor Elara Ursa's lecture. She learned that Wishlings were hopelessly behind in technology; their computers and communications devices were shockingly old-fashioned. In addition, their modes of transportation were slow and cumbersome, plus they actually had to be operated by Wishlings themselves! Oh, how the girls laughed when they saw the funny vehicles Wishlings used to travel. Life on Wishworld was very interesting indeed.

"Sage! Sage!" said a voice. Sage tore her gaze from her view of Wishworld and turned around reluctantly. Professor Elara Ursa was shaking her head. "I've been calling your name for five starmins!" she said. "Class is over!" Sage looked around, blinking. The Wishworld Observation Deck was deserted. She muttered her apologies and took off hurriedly for her next class. She slipped into the last remaining seat right before the teacher closed the door and turned around with a scowl. "My name is Professor Lucretia Delphinus and above all I value timeliness!" she announced. Her eyes flashed behind her large black glasses. She was small and intense and immediately began pacing the room.

Sage gulped. *Way to make a good first impression*, she thought.

"This is Wish Identification class," said the professor. "Once you arrive on Wishworld, blend in, and find your Wisher by using your Wish Pendant, the most difficult part of your Wish Mission begins—making sure you identify the correct wish. This is obviously quite critical to your mission and will be the difference between collecting wish energy and returning home empty-handed."

A student with long, straight midnight-blue hair and eyes the color of the sky at night raised her hand.

"Yes?" said Professor Lucretia Delphinus. She attempted to hop up to sit on the corner of her desk. As she was tiny, she didn't make it at first and had to try a couple of times. Finally, she dragged over a chair and used it to climb onto the desk. She settled herself, then stared at the girls as if daring them to giggle at her. The students, completely intimidated, did not.

"You had a question?" she asked the blue-haired girl.

The girl, nonplussed by her professor's odd behavior, stared for a moment. "Um, won't the wish be obvious?" she finally asked.

"Not necessarily," replied Professor Lucretia Delphinus. "Here's what happens: When you arrive on Wishworld, your Star-Zap will give you directions to find your Wisher. When you are near your Wisher for the first time, your Wish Pendant will light up. It will be faint when you are in their vicinity and glow brightly when you make actual contact. That is when you can start trying to identify the wish. This is very tricky, because there is often nothing to indicate that you are correct. It's just a feeling you have. Some very perceptive Starlings will get a burst of energy when the wish is identified, but many will not. This coupled with the short time frame to complete the wish results in a fifty percent failure rate."

Sage was shocked. She'd had no idea the failure rate was so high.

"My goal is to teach you how to ask the right questions, become more perceptive, sharpen your senses, and be good listeners," the professor continued.

"Have you ever identified a wish on the first try?" a girl in the front row asked.

Professor Lucretia Delphinus nodded. "Sometimes it is easy. Once I introduced myself to a Wisher and she said, 'Boy, you're friendly. I wish I could be as friendly as you.' And I knew that my mission was to build her confidence and help her make friends. But most times it is not so simple."

She put her hand to her chin. "On one mission I went on, I was fully convinced that my Wisher wanted to learn how to tap-dance."

"How to what-dance?" asked Sage.

Professor Lucretia Delphinus smiled. "It's a Wishling pastime in which they do special dances with very small metal plates attached to their shoes. Very noisy."

"So what was the real wish?" Sage asked.

"Her actual wish was to get the courage to tell her parents she wanted to quit taking piano lessons. Boy, did she hate them," Professor Lucretia Delphinus said, remembering. "I'm still not quite sure how I messed that one up. But luckily I discovered it in time." The next thing the class knew, she had hopped off the desk and started doing a strange shuffling dance. "And I did become quite the tap dancer!"

The professor finished the dance by extending her arms and shaking her hands, her palms forward and fingers splayed. "Jazz hands," she explained. The students just stared. Professor Lucretia Delphinus was certainly a character!

She cleared her throat and continued her lecture. "What makes wish identification so difficult is that the Wisher may have multiple wishes at the same time. They could even have several good wishes. So you must be sure to identify the correct wish. Here is why so many Wish Missions fail: the Starling assumes that the first wish they uncover is the correct wish. You really have to take the time to get to know your Wisher to make sure you grant the wish that is their heart's desire."

The students paid close attention. Wish granting was much more complicated than they had realized!

Professor Lucretia Delphinus looked at all the confused faces in front of her and softened. "Since it is your first day, we'll go back to the basics. We'll talk about good, bad, and impossible wishes. That will be a good way to ease into wish identification.

"So tell me this," Professor Lucretia Delphinus said. "What exactly makes a wish impossible?"

The arms of nearly half the class shot up. "Yes," said the professor, pointing to a girl with magenta hair.

"Wishes that are not within the Wishling's grasp," the girl answered.

"Good. Can I have some examples?" Professor Lucretia Delphinus asked.

Girls started calling out.

"Curing diseases!"

"Reading minds!"

"Flying!"

"All good examples," the teacher said with a nod. "We all wish that things like world peace and curing diseases were not impossible wishes.

"And how about bad wishes?" the professor prompted.

"Bad wishes are selfish," Sage said.

"Yes, anything else?"

"Bad wishes harm other people and don't take their feelings into consideration," offered another student.

"Correct," Professor Lucretia Delphinus said. "And last but not least, what is a good wish?"

"Good wishes are those made for something positive with no ulterior motives," Tweela said slowly.

Professor Lucretia Delphinus rubbed her hands

together. "Excellent, girls. Now let's try this: I am going to give you three wishes to choose from. Listen carefully and pick the wish which is not only good but is also possible." The girls nodded.

"Wish number one: a Wishling wants her coworker to perform badly at an upcoming presentation so that she will look better to their boss.

"Wish number two: a Wishling wishes for the courage to try out for the neighborhood baseball team." Puzzled expressions appeared, so Professor Lucretia Delphinus described an activity that involved a large padded leather glove, bats made of wood or aluminum, and something called a "home run," leaving the girls more confused than before.

"And wish number three: a Wishling whose grandmother is very sick wishes she could do something to make her all better."

A girl scoffed. "That's easy," she said. "It's the Wisher who wants to impress her boss."

"No, no, no," said the teacher, wringing her hands. "Why would wishing for another to fail be a good wish?"

The girl shook her head. "I think this is a trick question!" she said confidently. "It's about her job, so it has to be a good wish!"

Professor Lucretia Delphinus put her hand to her

head as if she had a sharp and sudden headache. "I see we have some work to do," she said. Sage agreed. It was pretty clear that while everyone seemed to know which wish was which in theory, when it was put into practice, it was an entirely different story.

Luckily for everyone, the bell rang. It was time to head to the next class of the day.

Sage was dismayed when she entered her Wishful Thinking class and spotted the girl with the pale blue bangs sitting in the front row. It turned out her name was Vivica, and—no surprise—she was a bit of an obnoxious know-it-all. Sage decided not to let it bother her. Wishful Thinking was an important class. Up until then, none of the students had had any formal training in wish energy manipulation. It was something you practiced at home with your family. Now that they were at the Age of Fulfillment, they were ready to hone their skills.

"As you know, positive wish energy is around us at all times. Not only does it power our lights and cars, but we can use it to manipulate things around us with our minds," said the teacher, a short, stern woman named Professor Dolores Raye. She wore sensible shoes with stars on them, and her illuminated glasses were on a glowstring around her neck so she wouldn't mis-place them. "We fully expect you all to be on markedly different levels. This is not a competition. By the end of the term, you will all be skilled manipulators. But first we have to assess your skills so we know where to begin."

As the class watched, the professor pointed to the classroom door, opening and closing it with ease. She stood up and, with a flick of her wrist, moved her chair across the room. She even lifted one student out of her seat and kept her floating in midair! Professor Dolores Raye was the most talented Wish Energy Manipulator Sage had ever seen. Even better than Gran. And Gran was really good.

"And now it's your turn," the teacher said. After that stunning display, no one was about to volunteer to go first. But finally, a girl with short-cropped violet hair was brave enough to try. Professor Raye placed a beautiful stone—a brilliant pink rodangular—on the desk and asked her to move it. The girl stared at the gem. Nothing. She frowned and her face began to turn red. Still nothing. She put her hands to her temples and concentrated fiercely. Then the gem began to tremble. It moved forward the tiniest bit. It was nearly imperceptible, but the girl looked happy. "Wonderful effort!" Professor Dolores Raye said. "Don't worry, it will only get easier."

Finally, it was last period. Sage spotted Cassie in the

hallway and caught up, falling into step beside her. "So how was your day?" Sage asked.

Cassie sighed. "I read my holo-schedule wrong and accidentally went to Astral Accounting class twice. It couldn't have been Aspirational Art or Lighterature, right? And now I am going to get in trouble for skipping Wish Identification class."

"With Professor Lucretia Delphinus?" Sage asked.

"Yes," replied Cassie.

Sage grimaced. Cassie probably *was* going to get in trouble.

"So how was your first day?" Cassie asked.

"It was intense," Sage said. "I kind of felt like my brain was going to explode. But otherwise it was okay."

"Where are you going, girls?" said someone behind them.

Oh, no, thought Sage. She recognized that voice and wished she didn't.

Sure enough, it was Vivica. She pushed in between the two roommates and started walking with them. "Pretty lame manipulation attempt today, wouldn't you say, Sage? Wait till it's my turn. Then you'll really see some skills."

"Sounds good," said Sage.

"So where are you two off to now?" Vivica asked, pushing her bangs out of her eyes. She smirked before adding, "Oh, that's right, you're part of the, um . . ." She searched her mind. "Superbly Dense group," she concluded with a nasty grin.

Sage stopped suddenly in the hallway, her temperature rising. Students had to step around her. Cassie and Vivica stopped, too, Vivica's expression mocking. *Why won't this girl leave me alone?* Sage wondered. She clenched her hands.

Cassie gently put her hand on Sage's arm. It had a sudden calming effect on her. She took a deep breath. "I can't put anything past you," Sage said to Vivica with forced cheerfulness. "Turns out I do need some extra help. She does, too," she added, pointing to Cassie, much to the girl's dismay. "Can't be late! Don't want to fall even more behind!" she said, taking off down the hallway, Cassie right behind her.

"Thanks a lot," muttered Cassie. "You actually had to *volunteer* that information?"

"It was going to get out sooner or later," said Sage.

"I guess you're right," said Cassie grudgingly. The two reached the classroom and stepped inside. They sat next to Vega, who was neat as a pin in her crisp blue outfit.

The girl with the fuchsia hair entered the classroom and sat in the corner by herself.

"That's Scarlet," Vega whispered to Sage. "And she's just weird. She totally keeps to herself. Super unfriendly."

The girl definitely had a look that was all her own. That day she wore a black T-shirt decorated with a star made out of silver studs, a pouffy black tutu, pink-and-black-striped tights, and big black boots. She didn't look at anyone, just gazed down at her desk.

The classroom filled up. Gemma entered, chatting away to her sister. Leona was the last student to arrive, gesturing dramatically with her hands.

Lady Stella and another teacher walked into the room. "Welcome, Star Darlings," the headmistress said. "For these special secret classes, we will have several guest lecturers, who will each present crucial information. Today we are lucky to have Professor Margaret Dumarre, who is here to teach you all we know about Wishling schools. Since we usually send older Starlings down to grant wishes, our knowledge of Wishling schools is limited. We will be relying on you to make Wishworld observations, which you can mentally record in your Cyber Journals as they happen and we will discuss in class upon your return. These will prove very beneficial to your fellow Star Darlings, as well as to the rest of Starling Academy."

"Hello, students," said Professor Margaret Dumarre with a warm smile. Sage was immediately charmed by the pretty young teacher. Her pink-and-blue-striped hair was twisted into an elegant updo, and she was wearing a sleek high-collared bright pink dress, scattered with glowing stars. "I already know some of you from my third-year course Wishworld Relations." Several of the older Star Darlings nodded.

Professor Margaret Dumarre began her lecture and reviewed for the Star Darlings that Wishling children weren't born with knowledge of basic concepts, the way Starlings were. They had to go to school to learn simple skills such as counting, spelling, and reading. The upperclassmen were familiar with that information, but the younger students, who had learned it only that day, were even more surprised to learn that Wishling children didn't absorb their lessons in their sleep.

Their mouths fell open in shock when they discovered that Wishling children actually read and studied books made of paper.

"Moons and stars!" Cassie exclaimed. "I would love to see one of those!"

When class was over, Professor Margaret Dumarre and Lady Stella stood at the door as the students filed out. "Excellent work today, girls," Lady Stella said. "And who knows? A wish could be coming through as I speak. One of you may be on your way to Wishworld before you know it!"

Sage tapped her elbows together for luck. She hoped Lady Stella was right.

CHAPTER
5

But it was not to be. Days turned into weeks and still there were no missions for the Star Darlings. Sage fell into a routine of classes, clubs, and regular calls home. She joined the holo-book club (at Cassie's request) and the explorer's club, which met every Reliquaday. She took her first hike to the Crystal Mountains, which were just as spectacular as she had imagined. And she finally read the Student Manual from start to finish, much to Cassie's and Gran's relief.

In her classes, Sage learned a lot about Wishlings and Star-Zaps and wish identification.

But Sage could never fully relax, knowing that she could be summoned for her mission to Wishworld at any moment. Some of the other Star Darlings seemed keyed up, as well. There was a wide range of emotions running through the group, as some of them just couldn't wait to get going and others were a bit more reluctant. Some pretended to be blasé even though they were nervous. But Cassie made it no secret that she was in no rush to head for Wishworld any time soon.

Lady Stella put on a brave face. "Everything is going as planned," she said often. "Your missions could start at any moment. Be ready." But Sage had spotted the Wish-Watcher who was in charge of the Star Darlings' Wish Orbs coming out of Lady Stella's office the past week looking very worried indeed.

Sage enjoyed Wishful Thinking class most of all, although she had not yet had her turn to showcase her talents. It was fascinating to see the different skill levels of the students.

One day she arrived in class early to find that she and Vivica were the only ones there. Sage quickly sat down and started fiddling with her Star-Zap. The next thing she knew, Sage looked up to discover Vivica leaning on her desk. She jumped. "So, how's everything going, Sage?" Vivica asked.

"Just fine," replied Sage guardedly.

"Glad to hear it. I'd hate to hear that you were over-whelmed or anything."

"I'm fine," said Sage. "Thanks for asking." When she had been in Wee Constellation School, there had been a boy in her class who picked on everyone smaller than him. When Sage had gone home crying because he had said she smelled like stinkberries, her mom had assured her she smelled lovely and then taught her how to deal with bullies—by simply ignoring them. It had worked with that boy, and Sage hoped it would work now. "Bullies want to get a reaction out of you," Indirra had told her. "It makes them feel powerful. Don't give him the satisfaction."

Some other girls came into the classroom, and then Vivica had an audience. She smiled a mean smile. "So how is your study group going?" she asked in a loud voice for the other girls' benefit. "Did you all know that Sage and her roommate are in an extra class?" The other girls didn't say anything, but a couple looked intrigued. Sage shifted in her seat. "Makes you wonder why she would be accepted into such a prestigious academy," Vivica continued. "Makes you wonder if she had some help getting in. Like maybe someone's well-known scientist mother pulled some strings and got her daughter into school."

"That's not true!" shouted Sage. *Starf!* She hadn't meant to let the mean girl get to her.

Professor Dolores Raye walked into the classroom at that very moment, of course. "Sage," she scolded, "no shouting in the classroom, please!"

Sage scowled and sunk in her seat till her head was barely at desk level. Great, now her favorite professor was mad at her. Sage was angry. And maybe—just maybe—the reason she was so angry was that she herself feared that there was some truth to what Vivica had said. She had been pleasantly surprised when she had been accepted to Starling Academy. Could that be the real reason she had been accepted? Was she an imposter?

After SD class that day, Sage was on her way back to her room when she spotted a dapper-looking gentleman chatting with a Bot-Bot guard on the Little Dipper Dormitory's steps.

"This is Cassie's roommate, Sage," the Bot-Bot guard informed the man as she approached.

"Star salutations," the man said to the guard. He turned to Sage and bowed. "Hello, Sage. I am Andreas. I'm here to see Cassie."

"She stopped to drop off some holo-books at the library," explained Sage. She looked up and noticed he had the same soft burgundy eyes as her roommate. She smiled. "You must be her father!" she cried. "It is so nice to finally meet you. Cassie is a great roommate! She even got me to join the holo-book club." She looked around. "Hey, is her mom here? I can't wait to meet her, too!"

Andreas looked confused. "No, I am Cassie's uncle." He frowned and leaned forward. "You do know that Cassie's parents have completed their Cycle of Life, don't you?" he said in a low voice. "Back when she was six years old. She has lived with me ever since. I am her guardian, her mother's older brother."

Sage stared. "You mean they have begun their afterglow?" she said. "But Cassie . . ." Suddenly, she realized that the holo-pictures displayed in their room were of a much younger Cassie and her parents. And she recalled how Cassie often stared into the heavens before bed. She had assumed her roommate had been on the lookout for shooting stars, but now she realized she must have been staring at her parents' stars. She felt a sudden stab of sorrow. Poor Cassie!

"Oh, there she is!" her uncle said, a smile on his face. "Cassie!" He waved and began heading over to her. Cassie's mouth opened into an O of surprise. She ran to her uncle, her arms outstretched.

Sage decided the kindest thing to do was slip away without Cassie seeing her. She headed in the other direction. She'd hang out in the Lightning Lounge until dinnertime to give her roommate some space.

Sage returned to the room as Cassie was drawing the curtains shut. "Sorry I didn't make it to dinner tonight," Cassie said. "My uncle Andreas came for a visit and he took me out to eat. My, um, parents were busy, so he came instead."

"Cassie," said Sage slowly, "I . . . um . . . met your uncle. He told me that your parents were . . ."

Cassie opened a drawer and was suddenly very busy picking out a pair of pajamas. "Oh," she said. "Oh, I see. Okay."

"If you want to talk about it, we can . . ."

Cassie quickly got changed and slid into bed. "No, it's okay. Good night." She slipped her headphones onto her ears and turned to face the wall.

Sage put on her own headphones and tried to fall asleep. But she couldn't. She felt terribly sad for Cassie, and also awkward. She lay awake watching the shadows on the wall. She was sure Cassie was awake, too.

When Sage woke up the next morning, the room was empty. Cassie's bed was perfectly made. Suddenly, Sage's Star-Zap lit up. A holo-text appeared. DEAR SAGE, it read, I'M SORRY I LIED TO YOU ABOUT MY PARENTS. I'M ACTU-ALLY NOT EVEN SURE WHY I DID IT. I GUESS IT'S JUST THAT

WHEN YOU ASSUMED THEY WERE AROUND, AND TALKED ABOUT THEM LIKE THEY WERE ALIVE, IT FELT REALLY GOOD TO GO ALONG WITH IT. IT WAS EASY TO PRETEND THAT WE WERE APART BECAUSE I WAS AT SCHOOL, AND NOT BECAUSE THEY HAD BEGUN THEIR AFTERGLOW. I LIKED PRETEND-ING THAT THEY WERE STILL AT HOME WAITING FOR ME. I'M SORRY FOR LYING TO YOU AND I'M REALLY EMBARRASSED TOO. YOUR ROOMMATE, CASSIE. PS: I'D APPRECIATE IT IF WE NEVER TALKED ABOUT THIS AGAIN.

DEAR CASSIE, Sage wrote back after much thought, NO NEED TO EVER APOLOGIZE TO ME. I'M THE ONE WHO IS SORRY. I PROMISE I'LL NEVER BRING IT UP AGAIN. LOVE, SAGE.

Now that the truth was out there, Sage learned a lot more about Cassie's life. Her uncle was a best-selling author who sold mooniums of holo-books a year. Sage's dad was a big fan of his mysteries. He traveled Starland extensively on book tours, and Cassie often accompa-nied him on his trips. If she didn't feel like going, she stayed at home (in a large mansion) with their house-keeper, Marta, a sweet older woman who was as close to Cassie as if she were her grandmother.

"No wonder you love books so much!" Sage said. She was delighted to learn that Cassie was also a recurring character in the series, as a brilliant young sleuth who often assisted the main character on cases. Now that Cassie's secret was out in the open, the two girls fell into an easy friendship.

Then one day everything changed. It was finally Sage's turn in Wishful Thinking, and she was very excited. She stood in front of the class. This time there were a pitcher of glorange juice and an empty glass on Professor Dolores Raye's desk.

The teacher called her name and Sage walked to the front of the room. "Okay, Sage, time to show us what you've got," said Professor Dolores Raye.

"Here goes nothing," said Vivica under her breath. The meaner girls in the class giggled.

Sage smiled. Now she would show everyone who was supposed to be at Starling Academy! She stared at the glass and it slid gracefully across the table.

"Well done, Sage," said Professor Dolores Raye with a broad grin.

For her next trick, Sage decided she would levitate the pitcher and pour the teacher a glass of juice. Sage was an expert at wish energy manipulation. She had been practically since birth. As a baby she had shocked her parents by levitating a toy across the room and float-ing it into her chubby little hand. She had been crying for it and they hadn't been able to understand what she wanted. So she simply concentrated on it, and there it was. This energy had also come in handy while she was learning how to glimmerskate. It had kept her from falling over.

But just as she was lifting the glass, her Star-Zap vibrated. *Probably just a holo-text from Gran*, she thought. She stole a glance at it.

SD WISH ORB IDENTIFIED, she read. PROCEED TO LADY STELLA'S OFFICE IMMEDIATELY.

CRASH! The pitcher fell to the floor and shattered. There were glass shards and glowing orange juice all over the floor. Then it was instantly gone.

"That was a good try, Sage," said the professor sympathetically.

Several girls laughed, and Vivica shook her head. But Sage didn't even notice. Her heart was fairly leaping out of her chest with excitement. She grabbed her Star-Zap and asked to be excused. Sage walked down the hall quickly, her heels clicking on the marble floor. A classroom door opened and Scarlet came out. She spoke to Sage for the first time ever. "It's happening," she said, her black eyes shining. "It is really happening. Right here, right now."

The two girls grinned at each other and ran down the hall toward the headmistress's office.

Once again, the girls sat around the table in Lady

Stella's office. Cassie looked even paler than usual. "I can't believe this is actually happening so soon," she whispered to Sage.

So soon? thought Sage. It felt like it had taken forever!

The door opened and Lady Stella strode inside. She looked energized and, Sage noted, slightly nervous. She stood in front of the girls and clasped her hands together. "This is it, Star Darlings: the moment we have all been waiting for. A Star Darling's Wish Orb has been identified by our Wish-Watcher. It is time for us to head to the Star Darlings Wish-Cavern to find out who the wish belongs to. Let's go underground."

Underground? The girls looked at each other in confusion.

"Deep underneath Halo Hall is a labyrinth of underground caves," Lady Stella explained. "They are secret—known only to a few members of the faculty. And now you. We decided to build your special Wish-Cavern there to keep its existence secret from prying eyes."

Lady Stella walked to her desk and opened a drawer. She reached inside and a hidden door in the back wall slid open. Sage was one of the first through the doorway and found herself descending a circular stairway. There was a sudden change in temperature and the air grew musty and damp. Sage shivered. The girls walked in silence, the only sound the echoing clatter of their footsteps on the metal stairs. Suddenly, someone started to sing. She sang softly at first; then the song grew louder. It was a pretty tune about stars twinkling in the darkness, and the voice was clear and sweet. Sage thought it might be Leona.

Finally, they reached the bottom of the steps, and the singing stopped. The only light came from the glowing rocks set in the dripping walls of the cavernous room they stood in. "Welcome to the Star Caves," Lady Stella said, her voice echoing. "We will head to the Wish-House in a moment. But first I want you to experience just how complete the darkness is down here. Are you ready?"

"Yes," said several voices. Sage thought she recognized Leona's as the loudest.

Lady Stella closed her eyes and all the lights were suddenly extinguished. It was so utterly dark that Sage held up her hand and couldn't see it. Sage felt a small, cold hand grab hers and knew instantly it was Cassie's. Sage squeezed her hand, for her own comfort as much as her roommate's. Just then, the star on the middle of Lady Stella's forehead began to glow, illuminating her lovely face. After a moment the lights turned back on again, to everyone's relief.

"Follow me," Lady Stella said. "The Wish-Cavern is ready for us."

Sage worked her way through the crowd so she was right behind the headmistress. She shivered in the damp air. She wished she had worn a sweater. A big cold drop of water hit her squarely on the shoulder. In the spooky half gloom, she could see rocky formations rising from the floor and dripping down from the ceiling like stone icicles. A sudden squeaking sound made her jump.

"Don't worry," said Lady Stella. "It's just a bitbat. They don't bite—unless they're hungry."

Sage nervously laughed along with the other girls. She hoped the headmistress was kidding, but she wasn't quite sure.

"Ah, here we are," said Lady Stella, stopping in front of what looked like a sheer stone wall. She concentrated and a section of the wall slid open. A secret entrance! To Sage's amazement, bright sunlight flooded out. The girls pushed inside, eager to be out of the damp gloom. "Welcome to the Star Darlings Wish-Cavern," Lady Stella said. "This magical place has been created just for you and your Wish Missions." Though they were deep underneath Starling Academy, the girls found themselves in a working Wish-House, the sun streaming in through the glass roof. Golden waterfalls of pure wish energy streamed down the sides. Sage smiled as she felt the immediate effects of the positive energy. There was grass underneath their feet and a row of Wish Orbs, their sparkly forms bobbing. Sage counted them quickly. Eleven. She noticed that Astra had kicked off her shoes and was scrunching her toes in the velvety-looking grass.

The girls gravitated toward a grass-covered platform in the middle of the garden and stood around it uncertainly. Sage stood between Clover and Gemma, who both looked excited, and across from Cassie, who was much more reserved.

Lady Stella then announced, "One of twelve Wish Orbs is glowing, which means that a wish is ready to be granted. It is the perfect match for one of you. The timing is wonderful, as your studies have progressed enough that you are all ready to make the trip to Wishworld. Now the Wish Orb will choose which of you is the best match for its wish." The headmistress pointed to the platform. "Are you ready?" The girls nodded.

Lady Stella clapped her hands. The room darkened, and a beam of light appeared and focused on the middle of the round platform. As the girls watched, the center of the platform opened and up popped a single Wish Orb. It floated in the air. As the girls watched, it slowly moved to the edge of the platform and began to circle around, pausing momentarily in front of each Star Darling as if deciding which girl it belonged to.

Sage stared at it, hoping that it belonged to her. She closed her eyes. *Me, me, me . . . please be me, me . . .* When she opened her eyes, the orb was floating in front of her.

Lady Stella reached out and plucked the Wish Orb out of the air. She turned to Sage, her eyes brimming with tears. "This is a historic moment," she said. "The very first Star Darling has been chosen. The Wish Orb belongs to you, Sage." Was it Sage's imagination, or did the headmistress look relieved?

Sage could hardly breathe. "It's really me?" she finally managed to squeak out.

"It's really you," said Lady Stella. "Congratulations, Sage. Now it is time to prepare for your Wish Mission."

The headmistress clapped her hands again. "When we get upstairs, the rest of you girls are dismissed. Sage, you come with me. We have a lot to do before you leave. By tomorrow morning you will be on your way to helping Wishworld!"

CHAPTER
6

"**Go back to that** cute striped jacket and that skirt with the folds in it," said Cassie. She was lying on her bed watching Sage flip through the options on the Wishworld Outfit Selector on her Star-Zap. Pants, shirts, vests, skirts, dresses, leggings, hats. All kinds of shoes—sneakers, flats, platforms, tall boots, short boots, booties. The choices were endless. Sage pressed the CHOOSE button and a new Wishling outfit instantly appeared on her body.

"Now spin," said Cassie. Sage did, and the pleated skirt stood out, floating in the air. "Oh, I really like Wishworld fashion," said Cassie. "Can you find it in white?"

Sage flipped through several more outfits before finally settling on a comfortable pair of blue pants and some lavender sneakers. On top she wore a lavender shirt with a glittery flutterfocus—make that a butterfly—on it and a cute cropped jacket. She registered her choice by pressing a button on her Star-Zap, then put on a lavender nightgown, soft as a cloud, and crawled into bed.

"Good night, Sage," said Cassie. "I'm really excited for you. And I'm also really relieved that it's not me." She yawned. "I'm sure you'll do great." Sage stared at the ceiling, her mind racing. In mere hours she would be on her way to a strange new place where she would have to fit in, find the right Wisher, identify the wish, and help make it come true. She shivered with anticipation.

★

Sage stood on the private Star Darlings section of the Wishworld Surveillance Deck, her heart beating fast, her eyes protected by a pair of special safety starglasses. Two Star Wranglers stood nearby with lassos made of wish energy in their hands. Their job was to catch a falling star as it passed by and attach Sage to it. Then they'd let go and she'd be flung into the heavens.

Sage thought she'd be nervous, but she felt oddly calm. The rest of the Star Darlings, however, were buzzing with excitement as they hugged her and wished her well.

Lady Stella called for everyone's attention. "I have some last-starmin details to share," she said. "When you enter Wishworld's atmosphere, your Star-Zap will signal that it is time to change your appearance. You must make sure that your hair, skin, and clothing blend in with the Wishlings.

"That means no sparkly skin, no vibrant hair color, no Starland fashions," the headmistress stressed. "You must always keep your true identity a secret. To let the Wishlings know of our existence would be disastrous. We would be overwhelmed by wishes—many of them selfish ones. It is imperative that we keep the balance just as it is."

Sage nodded. "I understand."

"And a reminder—you must pay careful attention to the Countdown Clock on your Star-Zap. The wish must be granted before the orb dies. The timing is different in each case. A starsec too late and the wish energy will be lost forever. And keep a careful eye on the energy levels of your Wish Pendant. You can use it to help make the wish come true by using your special power." Sage nodded. "But of course, you have to figure out what your special power is!" Lady Stella smiled at her. "And remember, you never want to completely run out of wish energy, in case of an emergency.

"I cannot stress to you how important it is that each of you collect your wish energy. We need every drop."

"No need to worry," Sage said confidently. "I can do this."

Lady Stella continued. "Due to Wishworld's atmosphere, we will only be able to monitor your wish energy reserves in your Wish Pendant and see how much time you have left on the Countdown Clock. We will not be able to communicate with each other."

Sage nodded again.

"Now where is Lady Cordial?" asked Lady Stella. At that moment, the door opened and the purple-haired woman emerged, out of breath and holding a rectangular lavender bag with two shoulder straps and a purple stuffed star hanging from the zipper. "This is a bag we created to look like the ones all Wishworld children carry. This will help you fit in." Sage took it and slipped it over her arm.

Lady Stella looked at Sage proudly. "I have total faith that your journey will be a success," she told her. She smiled gently at Sage. "One last thing—don't forget your Mirror Mantra. It has been chosen especially for you: *I believe in you. Glow for it!* Recite it when you feel like you or your Wisher need reassurance and strength."

"I believe in you," Sage repeated. "Glow for it!"

Then there was a flurry of embraces and farewells, and before Sage knew it, the star wranglers had lassoed a falling star and attached her to it. Before she could tap her elbows together for luck, she was jolted back as the star was released and took off like a shot. Next stop: Wishworld.

The only way for Sage to describe the ride through the heavens was that it was like being on the most exciting, fastest star coaster in existence. There were flashes of light and glimmers of starshine. She passed through a gray cloud and shivered. *Must be negative wish energy,* she thought. And as soon as her ride began, it was almost over. Mooniums of floozels covered in mere starmins. Sage was entering Wishworld's atmosphere.

Her Star-Zap began to flash. COMMENCE APPEARANCE CHANGE, it read. Sage accessed the Wishworld Outfit Selector and was instantly dressed in the Wishling clothing she had chosen.

Next she closed her eyes and held her Wish Pendant tightly. "Star light, star bright," she began to recite, "the first star I see tonight: I wish I may, I wish I might, have the wish I wish tonight." Immediately, her pendant began to glow, and a warm, pleasant feeling settled over her.

Sage first concentrated on her hair, envisioning plain, light brown braids. She then focused on her skin, imagining it to be smooth and dull. The warmth went away and Sage opened her eyes.

Looking down, she felt a small stab of disappointment when she saw that her hair was no longer its rich lavender hue. The light brown braids looked very dull indeed. She was surprised to see that there was a layer of sparkles on her skin. She gave herself a quick shake and the glitter fell off. She felt plain and unadorned. But now she would fit right in.

PREPARE FOR LANDING, the Star-Zap read. Sage screwed her eyes shut and braced herself as she fell to Wishworld. If any Wishlings happened to look up and spot her arrival, they would think they were witnessing a falling star—a particularly lovely one, at that.

She landed with a gentle thump and opened her eyes. She was sitting on a small grassy hill in the middle of a cluster of yellow and orange trees. The star sat beside her, sputtering. She took off her safety glasses and put them away. She'd need them for the return trip home. She'd also need the star. She reached out a finger and gently poked it. It was cool to the touch. With a smile, she began to fold it, as she had been instructed by Lady Stella, until it was the size of a small star-shaped wallet. She placed it in the zippered front pocket of her backpack, then slipped her arms through the straps. There! Now she looked just like a real Wishling!

She was all alone. The landing coordinates had been carefully chosen to avoid Wishling observation. The only sound was a strange yet lovely chirpy kind of music, which she soon discovered came from small winged creatures that sat in the branches of the surrounding trees.

"Take me to the Wisher I've come to help," she said into her communicator. It immediately gave her precise directions.

Sage walked for a bit until she found a pathway. As she walked she saw lawns, benches, and more trees and soon realized that she had landed in the middle of a park. She saw more of those winged creatures that were making the melodic sounds she liked so much, as well as some gray animals with bushy tails. They chattered at her as she passed.

Very soon after that, she started seeing Wishlings. She couldn't help staring at them, despite herself. They really did look remarkably like Starlings but with lusterless, non-sparkly skin and plain hair colors, though some of them embellished their appearances with bright clothing, accessories, or face paint. Some of the female Wishlings wore improbably high shoes. Many of the males had long strips of cloth tied around their necks. Some Wishlings rolled by on wheeled footgear. Others led furry animals of all shapes and sizes by long ropes. Sage vaguely remembered they were called dags, or something like that. Sage left the park and crossed a busy street.

She gaped at the oddly shaped wheeled vehicles and the Wishlings inside them. It was true—they were actually driving!

Several blocks later she reached her destination, a large redbrick building with a flag flying out front. Her Wisher's school. She felt her pulse quicken as she walked up the steps and pushed open the doors. The hallway was long, empty, and lined with small metal closets. She wrinkled her nose at the harsh sanitized smell in the air. WALK DOWN THE HALLWAY, TURN LEFT, AND GO UP THE STAIRS, the communicator instructed on-screen. Sage stepped forward confidently, hardly able to contain her excitement. Her adventure was about to begin.

Until a voice halted her. "Stop right there," someone said. The order echoed in the empty hallway.

Sage's heart dropped. Would her mission be over before it even began?

CHAPTER
7

Sage spun around. An adult male Wishling with dark brown hair and a green uniform was standing in the middle of the hallway, frowning at her.

"And what are you wearing? You know that jeans and sneakers aren't allowed in school. I'll have to write you up a detention slip!"

Sage looked down at her blue pants and her shoes. She pressed a button on her Star-Zap and made a mental note, which she knew would instantly be recorded in her Cyber Journal: *Mission 1, Wishworld Observation #1: Do not wear "jeans and sneakers" to school.* As the male Wishling began filling out the paper, Sage quickly pressed another button on the communicator and accessed the outfit changer. She was instantly wearing brand-new clothing, hopefully appropriate this time.

In her haste she hadn't been able to make an informed choice and hoped her outfit was a pretty one. The man looked up from his clipboard. "Like I said, no jeans or . . ." The man stopped talking when he took in her outfit. He blinked slowly. "Wait—what? I could have sworn . . ." He shook his head, flustered. "Well . . . then where is your hall pass?" he asked, bristling.

Sage bit her lip. What on Starland was a hall pass? She hadn't learned about that in school. Suddenly, the Wishling looked around, sniffing the air. "*Mmmmm,*" he said, a smile creeping over his face. "Angel food cake."

That gave Sage a moment to think. And then, to her surprise, she found herself looking deep into his eyes and saying: "My name is Sage. I am the new student in school."

His reaction both surprised and delighted her. He nodded, his face solemn, almost as if he was in a trance. "Yes," he said. "Your name is Sage. You are the new student in school." He took another sniff and closed his eyes for a moment. "Reminds me of the cakes my grandma baked for me and my sister after school. She used to let us lick the beaters when she was done. Go right ahead!"

Sage allowed herself a small smile of victory as she resumed walking down the hallway and moved up the stairs, her footsteps echoing. She added observation number two: *Find out what a hall pass is. Seems important.*

ARRIVAL AT DESTINATION, the Star-Zap spelled out. Sage paused in front of the classroom door, took a deep breath, smoothed her braids, and opened it. Twenty-five students swiveled their heads in her direction. Sage suddenly felt self-conscious for the first time. It was an unfamiliar feeling, and fortunately only a momentary one.

A pretty adult female Wishling with straight blond hair pulled back into a low ponytail came to the door in a red polka-dotted dress. "May I help you?" she asked. She had a puzzled expression on her face. Then she looked down the hallway and breathed in deeply.

"They must be baking carrot cake in the lunchroom. Delicious." She smiled a faraway smile. "I can almost taste my mom's cream cheese frosting."

This time Sage knew just what to do. She looked deep into the teacher's eyes. "I am Sage," she said pleasantly. "I am the new student in your class."

The teacher nodded, just as the man in the hall had. "You are Sage. You are the new student in my class," she repeated. She pointed to a desk halfway down the row closest to the windows. "Please be seated. I am Ms. Daniels, your teacher."

Mission 1, Wishworld Observation #3: Young Star Darlings clearly have some form of mind control over adults. Sage walked down the aisle as some of the students gave her curious glances. She looked down at her outfit, and her eyes widened in surprise. In her rush to change, she hadn't noticed that the outfit changer had selected a bright green-and-blue-striped top, an orange skirt, and bright yellow leggings. She looked down again. And red-and-purple shoes. She grinned. She looked like a rainbow! *Well, at least I'm very bright and cheerful,* she thought.

A couple of the students tittered as she passed.

"Class," said the teacher. "There's no need to be rude to our new classmate."

"Nice backpack," said a boy. "But why isn't it on your back?"

Sage looked down at the bag, which she was wearing on her chest.

"Oops," she said. "I guess I thought it was a frontpack!"

The class laughed. But in a nice way, like she had made a joke on purpose. Sage grinned. She was off to a good start, completely unintentionally.

Sage stepped over a boy's outstretched legs and slid

into the plastic seat, resting her arms on the desk that was attached to it. *Jon was here* was scratched into the surface. She waited for the seat to adjust. But it stayed the same—hard, plastic, and uncomfortable. That was observation number four: *Wishling chairs do not adjust.*

She glanced around the room, wondering which student was the Wisher. Her Wish Pendant was glowing faintly, proof that her Wisher was nearby. Was it the redhead with the freckles? The pigtailed blonde staring into space? The one with jet-black shoulder-length hair who was gazing at her curiously? It could be anyone!

Ms. Daniels resumed her math lesson. She took a red writing utensil and copied numbers and symbols on the smooth white surface that ran across the front wall of the classroom. "Now, who wants to take a stab at this equation?" she asked.

Sage sat up with interest. Would a student actually stab it? Now *that* would be an interesting observation! But to her disappointment, no one did.

"Come on, guys," said Ms. Daniels. "Someone come up here and show Sage here how good we are at long division."

No volunteers.

"Two hundred and ninety-one thousand, six hundred and six divided by three hundred and seventy-one,"

Ms. Daniels said. "Remember: Dirty Monkeys Smell Completely Bad. You must Divide, Multiply, Subtract, Compare, and Bring Dow—"

"Seven hundred and eighty-six," Sage said automatically. The students stared at her with looks of awe on their faces. Sage felt a flush of pleasure at being the center of attention, this time in a good way. "Sage, we must first raise our—" Ms. Daniels's voice broke off. She looked down at her book. "That's right," she said slowly. She wrinkled her brow. "How is that possible? Are you using a calculator?"

"A what-ulator?" asked Sage. The class giggled in unison.

Ms. Daniels narrowed her eyes, then looked down at her book again. "Fifty thousand, one hundred ninety-three divided by ninety-nine?" she said.

"Five hundred and seven," said Sage, though she was getting the feeling that she should just be keeping her mouth shut. She started to feel uncomfortable as she realized that everyone was staring at her even harder. Sage sank lower in her seat. All that attention couldn't be good. She was supposed to blend in, after all.

Ms. Daniels looked puzzled. "Ninety-two thousand, five hundred and forty-five divided by four hundred and fifteen?"

And even though every fiber of her being wanted to shout out the right answer, Sage forced herself to say, "Two hundred and twenty-two?"

Ms. Daniels nodded, clearly satisfied. "No, it's two hundred and twenty-three! You must have had the same math book in your last school. That's got to be it."

"That's right," said Sage.

Mission 1, Wishworld Observation #5: If you want to remain undercover at school, keep your star talents to yourself. No showing off, tempting though it may be!

CHAPTER 8

Boy, did Sage feel sorry for Wishling students. Their lunchroom was nothing at all like the Celestial Café. It was noisy and smelled funny, kind of like stink-berries. There were no tablecloths, no plush chairs, no deep carpeting to sink your feet into. No climate control. There wasn't a cloth napkin to be seen.

Where was a Bot-Bot waiter to take your order when you needed one? It was positively primitive: you had to grab a plastic tray, point to the food you wanted, and wait while a lady with a net over her hair scooped it up and handed it to you. She would have to tell Professor Elara Ursa all about it when she returned to Starland.

And the food—well, Sage's stomach churned when

she saw it. Nevertheless, she pointed to something called mac and cheese and received a dense orange square on a plate. Everyone else was grabbing containers from a large cool box, so Sage grabbed one, too.

Sage stood in the middle of the room, wondering where to begin her search for her Wisher, when someone called out, "Hey, new girl! Over here!"

Sage headed over to the wildly waving Wishling and found herself at a lunch table with a bunch of girls from her class: the redhead, the one with the blond pigtails, and the one with jet-black hair were among them. They all introduced themselves—Maria, Hailey, Jenna, Ella, and Madison. Sage nodded and smiled at them. Now she was getting somewhere.

"You're really good at math," said the freckled redhead, whose name was Jenna. "You made it look like a piece of cake!"

"It looked like . . . cake?" Sage asked, confused. "What kind?"

The Wishling laughed, thinking Sage was making a joke.

"Yeah, you really did make it look easy," said Maria, who had shoulder-length dark hair and pretty brown eyes.

Sage nodded and smiled. *Mission 1, Wishworld Observation #6: Add "piece of cake" to the Wishling dictionary. It means "easy."*

"I like your outfit," said Hailey, the blonde with the pigtails. "Very colorful!"

"Thanks," said Sage. She picked up a box labeled CHOCOLATE MILK from her tray. "Ah, chocolate," she said, remembering her first Wishers 101 class. "It must be Valentine's Day!" She felt pleased to have made the connection. She was a little worried because Professor Ursa warned it would taste terrible.

The girls stared for a moment, then burst into laughter. "You are so funny!" cried Maria.

Sage shrugged. She turned the box upside down, studying it. She had no idea how to open it. They hadn't gotten to beverages in her Wishers 101 class.

The Wishlings started laughing again. "You can divide huge numbers in your head, but now you're acting like you're from another planet!" said Madison, a thin Wishling with super-short light brown hair.

Sage gulped. *Oh, starf!* Did Madison really know that she wasn't from Wishworld? What was she going to do? The Wishlings laughed and laughed. "Do you ever stop joking?" Madison asked. Sage suddenly realized that they were kidding. She sighed with relief.

Maria reached over and grabbed Sage's container, tore a short plastic tube off the back of it, and stabbed it into the box. "Here you go," she said, handing it back to Sage.

Still confused, Sage took it, then hesitantly put the tube into her mouth and drank. Her eyes widened. The drink was cold, sweet, rich, and improbably delicious. Professor Elara Ursa couldn't have been more wrong about chocolate. It was the best thing she'd ever tasted.

Madison laughed. "You act like you've never had chocolate milk before!" she said.

Sage grinned. Little did she know!

"Are you thinking what I'm thinking?" said Jenna. The rest of the girls nodded. They suddenly started whispering among themselves.

"So listen, new girl," said Jenna. "We think you're funny and we've decided to invite you to sit at our lunch table. Permanently."

Sage stole a glance at her Wish Pendant. It was still only faintly glowing. So none of these girls was her Wisher. But it meant she must be nearby.

"Thanks," she said.

"Here are some things you need to know to survive in Ms. Daniels's class. Joey Peterson picks his nose. So don't ever touch his hands if you can help it. Ms. Daniels gives surprise spelling quizzes every Friday, so be prepared."

"Molly Chow brings in the best birthday treats, so be nice to her and you'll always get seconds. And whatever you do, stay away from Genevieve," offered Hailey.

"Who's Genevieve?" Sage asked.

"Just the meanest girl in class," said Maria.

"The meanest girl in school," Ella said, correcting her. "She's over there in line in the pink dress."

"She's also the most spoiled girl in school," added Maria. "She's so mean I heard that she made this girl cry because she didn't like her outfit. You don't get much meaner than that!"

"That's pretty mean," agreed Sage.

"Well, you're a lot of fun," said Jenna. "Friendly." She made a face. "Not like that *other* new girl," she added.

"Who?" Sage asked.

"Jane," Hailey answered. "She's just so weird. She's like the complete opposite of you. It's like she thinks that *we* should be going out of our way to get to know *her*."

"She ignores us at school for an entire month but then expects us all to come to her birthday party. That takes a lot of nerve," added Jenna.

Sage sat up straight. *Interesting.* "So none of you are going to her party?" she asked.

"No way," said Ella. "Like, try to make friends with me first. I'm not just going to show up at your party when I don't know you."

"I bet she wishes you would all go to her party," Sage mused aloud.

"Well, she's going to keep wishing," said Hailey. Sage stood up, her heart racing with excitement. Could she have figured it out so quickly?

"The bell hasn't rung yet," said Maria. "Where are you going?"

"I'm going to say hello to Jane," she said. "Where is she?"

"Over there, by herself. As usual," said Ella, pointing to a table across the room. "Tell her we say hello!"

That sent the Wishlings into further peals of laughter.

Sage took that moment to head across the room. Jenna stopped laughing. "Wait," she said. "She's serious."

Sage stood at the head of the table where a female Wishling with long brown hair pulled back into a ponytail sat hunched over a book, eating a sandwich, her brow furrowed in concentration.

Sage studied her. Was she deeply engrossed in what she was reading or deeply engrossed in looking busy?

"Hey," Sage said. "Is this seat taken?"

Jane looked up, frowning at Sage's lame joke. "You're kidding, right? Not funny."

"Sorry," said Sage, leaning a hand on the table. "So, we're in the same class, huh? Any tips for the even newer girl?" She put her elbows on the table and rested her chin in her hands.

"You seem to be doing just fine," said Jane coldly. "Look at you, first day at school and you already have more friends than I do after a month."

Because I'm friendly, Sage thought. But she kept it to herself. She took a deep breath and plunged right in. "So, I hear you're having a birthday party."

Jane closed her book with a bang. "It's my mother's fault!" she exclaimed. "I didn't even want to have one. But she convinced me to invite almost every girl in the class. And then no one RSVP'd. Not a single person. Talk about humiliating! Now I'm the class loser and things are worse than ever."

"Well, I'd like to come," said Sage gently. "I love parties."

There was a momentary flash of excitement in Jane's eyes. But then her eyes narrowed. She turned away.

"Leave me alone," she said.

Sage blinked. "What did you say?"

"I said leave me alone," Jane repeated. She scowled. "I bet those girls just sent you over here to make fun of me, didn't they?"

"They didn't, I swear!" said Sage. She put up her hands and took a step backward while stealing a glance at her Wish Pendant. It was brightly lit. *Yes!*

"Oops," she said as she bumped into a passing student. "Pardon me."

"Ouch," said the student. "My foot!"

Sage turned around to see who it was. *Oh, great. Genevieve.*

"Sorry," said Sage.

"Whatever," said Genevieve with a shrug. She looked Sage up and down. "Hey, nice outfit."

Sage narrowed her eyes. She knew what Genevieve was up to. She was being sarcastic! Sage gave the girl a mean look. Genevieve stared back, about to say something. Then she walked away.

Mission 1, Wishworld Observation #7: There are mean kids everywhere—no matter what star you are on.

She turned back to her Wisher. "So would you say that you wish that people would come to your party?" she asked—quite cleverly, she thought.

"Didn't we cover that already?" Jane asked.

Sage pressed on. "Would you say that it is your heart's desire?"

Jane looked at Sage to see if she was serious. "Yeah, I guess it is," she admitted.

"Well, I really want to come to your party," Sage told Jane. "In fact, I want to help you throw the best party ever. A party so great that every Wish—I mean, girl in the class is going to beg to come."

"Everyone except for Genevieve," said Jane. "She's not invited." The scowl disappeared from her face and was replaced by a hopeful expression. "Do you really think people will come to my party?" she said softly.

"I really do," said Sage, nodding.

Now all I have to do is help Jane convince the rest of the female Wishlings in the class to come, she thought. *This is going to be a piece of pie.*

Sage felt very pleased with herself, already using a Wishling expression on her first day. *Hey, I'm a natural!* she thought. Everything was falling into place perfectly. The only thing left was to figure out *how* she was going to help make the wish come true. But the hard part was done. Professor Lucretia Delphinus would be proud.

CHAPTER
9

"There is no way I am going to Jane's birthday party," Jenna said, slamming her locker door and jamming the lock closed. She spun around, a scowl on her pretty face. "She's just not nice!"

Sage shook her head. "Listen, Jane actually *is* really nice. I think she just seems strange because she's too shy to talk to you guys."

Jenna shrugged. "Fine, I believe you," she said. Sage felt excited for a starsec. "But I still don't want to go to her party," she concluded.

Sage was flummoxed. Then she had an idea. She held her Wish Pendant in her hand. Maybe her special talent was young Wishling mind control. She looked deeply into Jenna's eyes. "You are going to Jane's party," she said. "You will tell all your friends to come, too."

Jenna stared back at Sage for a moment. "Whatever you say, Sage."

Sage grinned.

Jenna snorted with laughter. "You didn't think I was serious, did you? As if! Oh, Sage, you're so funny!"

So young Wishling mind control is not my special talent, thought Sage. *I wonder what it could be?*

Sage's heart sank. Jenna was the ringleader. If she didn't go, the rest of her friends wouldn't, either. "Is there something that would change your mind?" she asked pleadingly. "Anything you can think of?"

"No," said Jenna. But she had a funny look on her face. Sage had a feeling there was something that would convince Jenna. On a whim, she held her Wish Pendant and concentrated on the girl's thoughts to see if she could read them. She could! She had discovered her talent! Starmendous!

Jenna's thoughts flooded into Sage's mind: *Got to finish that math homework before volleyball practice. . . . Where's my notebook? . . . Wonder if Mom is making fried chicken tonight. . . . Sage has cool hair. . . . I would go to that party if they did something cool. So sick of those boring baby parties with piñatas and musical chairs. . . . Where is that notebook?*

Wow! It worked! Sage felt exhausted and she glanced

down at her Wish Pendant to see that the energy level had been seriously depleted. And she had no idea what Jenna meant—musical furniture? A pin-whatta? But it didn't matter. She knew how to make Jane's wish come true now.

Sage marched down the hallway, where she found Jane kneeling in front of her locker, shoving books into her backpack.

"Hey," Jane said to Sage. "I was looking for you. Want to come over and help me plan my party?"

"Great idea!" said Sage.

Jane zipped her bag and stood up. "I saw you talking to Jenna," she said eagerly. "Did she say she'll come?"

"I'm working on it," replied Sage.

They left the school together and walked down the sidewalk side by side. Fallen leaves crunched pleasantly under their feet. "Nice neighborhood," said Sage. The lawns were well manicured and the houses were large and imposing.

"This is the fancy part of town," Jane explained. "That's where Genevieve lives." She pointed to a particularly large home with a curved driveway.

"What's that little house for?" asked Sage, pointing. It had four doors but no windows.

Jane giggled. "Oh, Sage, you're so silly. You know that's the garage!"

"Uh, right," said Sage. "So, Genevieve seems pretty mean."

"That's what everyone says," replied Jane. "So I guess it must be true, right?" She shrugged. "I don't want to take any chances, so I just avoid her."

She glanced at Sage. "I love your lavender streak," she said. "I wish my mom would let me dye my hair."

Sage touched her hair. She hadn't realized she had a streak of lavender. If Jane liked the streak, imagine if she could see what Sage's real hair looked like.

"So, where are you from?" Jane asked Sage.

Sage had a moment of panic. "Oh, um . . . from far away," she answered.

Jane nodded. "Me too!" she said. "We moved all the way from Connecticut."

Sage hid a smile. "It's hard to be the new girl," she said.

"Tell me about it," said Jane.

Sage kicked a pebble as the two girls walked together in silence.

"Hey," Sage said suddenly. "Do you have any chocolate milk at your house?"

★

Jane's mom, Mrs. Newman, was positively beaming when her daughter arrived home with a friend.

"It is so lovely to meet you, Sage!" she gushed. "I'm so happy to meet one of Jane's new friends!" She turned to her daughter. "See? I told you it was only a matter of time!"

"*Moooom,*" groaned Jane, looking completely humiliated. Sage understood how Jane felt. Wishworld moms were remarkably similar to Starland moms—totally concerned about their kids while being utterly oblivious to how self-conscious their kids could be. Mrs. Newman hovered over Jane, tucking a stray piece of hair behind her daughter's ear. Jane swatted at her mother's hand good-naturedly. A wave of homesickness washed over Sage and she suddenly missed her family.

"So, let's get down to business," Sage said, more sharply than she intended.

Jane raised her eyebrows. "Okay," she said. "Where do we start?"

"We need to plan a"—Sage used a Wishworld expression she had overheard in the cafeteria line—"totally awesome party."

Jane nodded. "Okay. How about—"

"I have an idea!" interrupted Jane's mother, an

excited grin on her face. "How about an old-fashioned party, like from when I was a girl? You know, pin the tail on the donkey, musical chairs, bobbing for apples . . ."

"No!" shouted Sage, recalling Jenna's thoughts.

Jane and her mom gaped at her.

"I mean, great idea, but that's been done before," Sage explained quickly. "Let's be different. Unique!"

"How about a magician?" asked Mrs. Newman. "Or a funny clown who makes balloon animals?"

Sage stole a quick glance at Jane. The look of horror on Jane's face told her all she needed to know.

"*Mooooom*," said Jane. "We're not, like, three years old." She leaned over and whispered to Sage, "Let's go up to my room and plan in private."

Sage nodded with approval at Jane's bedroom. It was very tidy; her bed was made and her stuffed animals were neatly arranged on it. Sage spotted a shelf full of actual paper books. She carefully removed one and held it in her hands. She ran her fingers over the smooth cover. It was stark—black and red and white—with a picture of two girls in fur caps and capes standing on a snowy hill, with three snarling wolves below them. After a moment she lifted the cover and flipped through the thin pages. "Wow," she said.

Jane laughed. "You act like you've never seen a book

before!" she said. She looked over Sage's shoulder. "*The Wolves of Willoughby Chase*," Jane said. "It's so good. A fancy English manor. Two cousins. An evil governess. A terrible orphanage." She sighed. "It's one of my favorite books of all time."

"It sounds really exciting," said Sage.

Jane smiled. "Keep it. I've got another copy."

Sage carefully placed the book in her backpack. When she turned back around, she spotted something colorful lying on top of Jane's bookshelf. It was a pretty T-shirt, with a multicolored heart in vibrant pinks, purples, and blues. "What's that?" she asked curiously.

"Oh, it's just a T-shirt I made," said Jane offhandedly. But Sage was intrigued. She gazed at Jane's creation, taking in the bright colors, the artful placement of glitter.

"You made this?" Sage said. "It's beautiful."

Jane laughed. "I've got a dozen of them." At Sage's look of surprise, she shrugged. "I've had a lot of free time on my hands since we moved here!"

"Amazing," said Sage.

So Jane taught Sage how to make her very own gorgeous, glittery T-shirt. Sage tore different colors of crepe paper into small pieces, arranged them into a star shape (of course), and sprayed the pieces carefully with a water bottle filled with a pungent liquid called white vinegar. The wet paper left colorful shapes on the T-shirt. Jane then hit the shirt with a blast of glitter spray.

"You did a great job," said Jane when they were done and Sage's T-shirt lay drying on the desk. "Just wait till it dries."

"Thanks," said Sage. "You're a good teacher!" She held out her multicolored hands and wiggled her fingers, just like her professor had shown them.

"Jazz hands!" said Sage.

Jane laughed. "Oops, I forgot to give you gloves!" said Jane.

"Never mind," said Sage. "They're kind of pretty, in a weird way!"

"That was fun," said Jane. Then she sighed. "But we still don't have a plan for my birthday. Can you please stay for dinner so we can keep working on it?"

Sage touched the hem of her still-damp T-shirt and smiled. "Don't worry," she said to Jane. "I've got it all figured out. And I'd love to stay for dinner."

★

Jane's father sat at the head of the dining room table and sniffed the air. "Are we having pineapple upside-down cake for dessert tonight?" he asked hopefully. "It smells so good!"

"No," said Mrs. Newman. "We're having ice cream." She wrinkled her brow. "That's funny. I smell cake, too. But it smells like chocolate to me."

Sage stared at them. This was getting weird. "Please pass the . . . food," she said.

Mr. Newman chuckled. "You mean the spaghetti and marinara sauce? Sure!"

Sage finished two bowls of spaghetti. It was awkward to eat, but it was delicious!

For dessert they had something called strawberry ice cream. It was cold, sweet, and a lovely shade of pink.

After draining her third glass of chocolate milk, Sage volunteered to help clean up. As soon as she and Mrs. Newman were alone in the kitchen, Sage turned to her. "I have an idea," she said, looking deep into the woman's hazel eyes. "Why don't I sleep over at your house tonight?"

Jane walked in, holding a handful of forks, knives, and spoons, which she dumped into the sink with a clatter.

"I have an idea," Mrs. Newman said to Sage. "Why don't you sleep over at our house tonight?"

Jane's face lit up as she wiped her hands on a dish towel. "Really?" she said, giving her mom a quick hug around the middle. "That would be great." She grabbed

Sage's arm and steered her out of the kitchen and up the stairs. "My mom must really like you," she said. "She never lets me have sleepovers on a school night!"

After deciding to wear their new T-shirts to school the next day, the two girls did their homework (which Sage finished with impossible speed) and got ready for bed. Sage headed to the bathroom to slip into a nightgown she had borrowed from Jane. She turned to the mirror and stared at her transformed Wishling-looking self. Then she recalled Lady Stella's parting words to her: *Don't forget your Mirror Mantra!* She could use a jolt of positivity. But what was it?

Sage closed her eyes and searched her memory. Then she opened them, reached up, touched the mirror, and said: "I believe in you. Glow for it!"

Sage gasped as her reflection suddenly transformed. Her hair was its usual bright lavender, her skin was sparkly, and her eyes were clear violet once more. She looked down and saw that her braids were still light brown, then looked up again to admire her true self. She felt both rejuvenated and at peace.

There was a knock on the door. "Sage, are you almost done in there?" Jane called out. Sage jumped, grateful she had locked the door behind her. Imagine if Jane could see Sage's true self. That would be so dangerous!

"Just a star— I mean, a minute," Sage called. She quickly got changed, then headed to the door and shut off the light, giving her reflection one final glance.

She climbed into the low bed that pulled out from under Jane's bigger one and drew the covers up to her chin.

"Hey, Sage?" Jane whispered in the dark. "Do you really think people are going to come to my party?"

"I do," said Sage. "I really do."

Jane sighed. "I'm just not sure. Things were so much easier at home. I wish we'd never moved. I miss my old life."

"I know what you mean," said Sage. Now that her brain wasn't racing a moonium floozels a starmin, she realized she felt a tiny bit homesick. Sage could hear Jane shifting under the covers.

"I guess I thought it was going to be easy," Jane continued. "I had so many friends in my old school. I was really popular. Everyone always wanted to come to my birthday parties. I don't know. I just expected that people were going to want to be my friend, so I didn't even try. I'm kind of shy, you know." She sighed. "Maybe I missed my chance. Maybe it's too late."

"I don't think it's ever too late to make friends," said Sage. "I think everything is going to turn out okay. Just be yourself tomorrow—friendly and kind."

"Okay," said Jane. "I hope you're right. Good night."

"Good night, Jane." *I hope I'm right, too,* thought Sage before she drifted off to sleep. *Because if I am, everyone is going to be so proud of me.*

She rolled over. *Oh, and because I'll be helping save Starland, too, of course!*

CHAPTER
10

"**Ohmigod!** Where did you get that T-shirt?" Jenna squealed. "It's supercute!"

"Oh, this?" said Sage, holding back a grin. Things were going exactly as planned. She just wished she didn't feel so tired. There must be something in Wishworld's atmosphere that was sapping her strength. She was wearing her brand-new T-shirt over a turquoise long-sleeved shirt, with a lavender skirt, lavender-and-turquoise-striped tights, and lace-up boots.

It had taken a dozen tries with the outfit changer in the privacy of Jane's bathroom to pull together the perfect look. But she looked great, no doubt about it. If Jane was surprised that Sage hadn't asked to borrow clothes, she didn't mention it. Maybe young Wishlings always packed extra outfits in the backpacks they carried. Sage would have to look into that.

"Yes!" Jenna said. "It is fab-u-lous!"

The rest of the girls left their lockers ajar and gathered around Sage, admiring her outfit.

"Did you get it at the mall?" asked Maria.

The what? thought Sage. "Believe it or not, you can make one yourself," she said. "As a matter of fact, I'll be giving lessons . . ."

"Awesome!" said Hailey. "Just tell us when and where."

". . . with my friend Jane at her birthday party this Saturday," Sage finished. "She taught me how to make it. Right, Jane?"

Her eyes shyly downcast, Jane sidled across the hallway in her own colorful T-shirt. Hers was even more vibrant than Sage's. "Right," she said softly.

There was an awkward silence. The girls' eyes went back and forth as they glanced at one another.

"I totally forgot to RSVP," Jenna finally said. "Jane, can I still come?"

"Yeah," said Maria. "It's not too late, is it?"

Jane couldn't keep the smile off her face. "No, not too late at all," she said happily.

Sage noticed that Jane sat up straighter and even raised her hand a few times in class that morning. Her confidence was growing. Ms. Daniels was delighted. "Great job today, Jane," she said as the class filed out of the room. "Keep up the good work!"

Sage must have looked as tired as she felt, because the gym teacher let her sit in the bleachers for gym. She had a front-row seat for class, where she noted that Ella chose Jane to be the first one on her team. It turned out that was a wise choice: Jane was very good at the game they were playing. It was called dodgeball, and it didn't seem that fun at all to Sage. But Jane loved it: she got player after player out with her throws and caught the ball every time it was aimed at her.

When it was down to Jane and a young male Wishling with a crew cut from the other team, she threw the last ball low at her adversary with deadly accuracy. It ricocheted off his foot, winning the game for her team. She looked positively thrilled as her teammates pounded her on the back in congratulations.

At lunch, Sage and Jane grabbed trays and made their selections. Sage took two chocolate-milk boxes this time. They started to head to the other side of the lunchroom to Jane's usual table. "Hey, Jane! Sage! Over here!" cried Jenna. "Sit with us!"

Jane's eyes were shining as they made their way to Jenna and her friends. Sage felt a swell of pride for how close she was to completing her mission, and she checked the Countdown Clock on her Star-Zap. *Plenty of time*, she thought confidently.

"Sit next to me, Jane," Jenna commanded. She didn't even wait until Jane was seated before she exclaimed, "So, tell us more about your party! We can't wait!"

"I've been thinking about making a tie-dyed birthday cake!" said Jane. "What do you guys think?"

"Awesome!" several voices chorused.

Sage grinned. That was news to her. It *was* an awesome idea.

My work here is done, thought Sage. *Well, almost.* But her victorious feeling did not last long. "Uh-oh, look who's headed our way," said Ella.

Sage froze for a moment, then turned around. As she feared, it was Genevieve. Despite her apprehension, Sage couldn't help admiring the fluffy white sweaterdress the girl was wearing. It was soft and cozy-looking, with a draped collar. Genevieve's feet were clad in navy blue ankle boots; one tapped impatiently against the cafeteria floor once she came to an abrupt stop at the group's cafeteria table.

As Sage turned around to face her, she felt a sudden burst of energy. *That's odd*, she thought.

Genevieve looked from Sage to Jane and back again. "Oh, look, the two new girls are wearing matching shirts. How cute," she said.

Everyone gazed at Genevieve in silence.

Sage smiled. "Star sal—I mean, thank you," she said.

But Jenna scowled. "My mother always says if you don't have anything nice to say, don't say anything at all."

Genevieve looked pained. "But I"—she took a deep breath—"I have an idea. . . ."

Suddenly, Sage realized what was going on. Genevieve was being sarcastic again! She was making fun of Jane and messing up Sage's plan.

Sage felt her cheeks getting warm. She could hear Gran's voice saying, *Take a deep breath before you speak, Sage. You can choose a better response!* But she didn't listen. She stood up and faced the girl. "I have an idea, too," she said. "Why don't you leave us alone?"

Genevieve's face sort of crumpled. "Fine," she said. But then she suddenly glanced down and shrieked. "Look what you've done!"

Sage looked down . . . and realized she had been clenching her box of chocolate milk in her angry hands, squeezing its contents all over Genevieve's sweaterdress. It was a complete and utter mess. To her dismay, the girls at the table—everyone except Jane—erupted into laughter.

Mission 1, Wishworld Observation #8: Wishling clothing really does stain.

"You ruined my cashmere dress!" Genevieve yelled. She looked as if she was going to cry. Sage sat down, defeated and embarrassed. Her red-hot anger had disappeared as quickly as it had surfaced, replaced by an overwhelming feeling of sorrow. Genevieve spun on her heel and stormed off, her golden bracelets jangling.

"Don't worry about her," said Jenna. "She deserves it. She's so mean. Besides, her parents can just buy her a whole closetful of new dresses."

But Sage felt terrible anyway. And she felt dreadfully tired—so tired she could hardly force herself to stand when the end-of-lunch bell rang. *Oh well, at least my mission is under control,* she thought.

Jane was visiting her grandmother that night, so the two girls said good-bye after school. "Come to my house early tomorrow!" Jane called, and Sage promised she would. Sage headed back to the park where she had landed. She was excited to use the special tent that Lady Stella had told her about. When she got to the park, she reached into her backpack and pulled out her Star-Zap to project her special tent. Before her unbelieving eyes appeared a large, luxurious sleeping quarters. It was invisible to Wishlings and once inside, Sage herself was undetectable. She was pleased to realize that it contained anything she would need—food, light, holo-books, and her favorite blanket. It was warm, comfortable, and extremely cozy.

Later that night, tired as she was, Sage couldn't fall asleep. She just couldn't shake the nagging feeling that something wasn't quite right. Sage opened the tent flap and gazed up at the heavens.

Suddenly, a falling star illuminated the night sky with a flash of brilliant light. A feeling of peace swept over Sage, and she smiled. Comforted, she closed her eyes and fell into a deep and dreamless sleep.

CHAPTER
11

It had been a very busy morning, but everything was almost ready, and the backyard looked perfect. The tables were covered with brightly patterned tablecloths and jars full of eye-popping displays of wildflowers. The tree branches were twinkling with fairy lights, and paper lanterns hung between the trees.

A colorful banner, with a letter on each triangular flag, spelled out HAPPY BIRTHDAY, JANE! A fun photo booth was set up in a corner with a polka-dotted backdrop and silly paper props like hats and fake eyeglasses. Jane's mother was heating up the grill, and her father was practicing playing DJ—and he was actually pretty good. Jane bustled about, setting up the "make your own tie-dyed T-shirt" table. She looked up at Sage. "Hey, the guests are going to be here in fifteen minutes! Go get dressed!"

Sage looked down at her dusty T-shirt. "Good idea!" she said with a laugh. She headed upstairs, glancing down at her Star-Zap. Seventy-five starmins to go on the Countdown Clock. Talk about cutting things close!

Sage took a last look around Jane's bedroom as she packed up her backpack. These Wishling artifacts—her notebook and pencils from school, her math book, and the paperback that Jane had given her—would be of real interest to her Wishers 101 teacher, Professor Elara Ursa.

Sage put on her tie-dyed shirt. She used her outfit changer to select a pretty lavender skirt, turquoise leggings, and lavender flats with big flowers on them. Just as she finished brushing and braiding her hair, the doorbell rang. She bounded downstairs and opened the door with a smile.

"Welcome to Jane's . . ." She blinked in surprise. "OMS, what are *you* doing here?"

In front of her was a familiar face—Tessa! Sage blinked at her in surprise. "How . . . what . . . but you're sparkly! And your hair is still green!" Sage managed to get out. Tessa was as shimmery and vibrant as she was

at home. Tessa grinned. "You look sparkly, too," she told
Sage. "I think we can see each other as we actually are."

"Aren't you going to invite me in?" asked Tessa.

"Why are you here?" Sage said huffily. "Everything's
fine. The party is about to start. I'm just going to collect
my wish energy and come back home."

Tessa smiled. "Sage, relax. I'm sure it's no big deal,
but Lady Stella thinks that something might be a little
off with your mission. Your wish energy levels were getting low so she sent me down to check things out," she
said. "Your vital signs were worrying her. It was pretty
clear that your strength levels were falling. And that is
the classic sign of a mission gone wrong."

Sage shook her head. "So I'm a little tired. So what?
Look, as soon as the first guest arrives, the wish will
come true. The Countdown Clock will stop. You'll see."

Just then Jane came in.

"Hey, Sage, tell me if I'm just being crazy . . ." Her
voice trailed off. "Hello!" she said. "Sage, I didn't know
you invited a friend!"

"Yes," Sage said quickly. "I hope that's okay. This is
my friend Tessa."

"No, that's awesome!" said Jane. "Pleased to meet
you, Tessa. The more the merrier. Make yourself at

home. We have tons of food and extra T-shirts you can make." She pulled Sage aside. "I'm just freaking out a little," she said softly. She pointed at her T-shirt. "I wish the shirts were fancier. Doesn't it feel like something is missing?"

"Oh, don't be silly," said Sage. "They're perfect just the way they are."

"I guess you're right," Jane said with a sigh. "I just wish they were a little cooler-looking."

The doorbell rang. "The guests are here!" Jane squealed. She ran to the front door to let them in.

Sage held up her Star-Zap. "Now watch," she said. "The clock is going to stop. Her wish has been granted. The guests are here."

Tessa shook her head. "Something's wrong," she said.

"Just wait," said Sage.

"Ella! Madison!" cried Jane. The two girls looked like special party editions of themselves. Madison wore a headband with a huge flower on it, and Ella had on a pair of glittery shoes. They hugged Jane hello and handed her their gifts. They waved to Sage as Jane ushered them through the house and into the backyard.

Sage gulped as the numbers kept ticking by. She could not believe her eyes. The wish had been fulfilled—there were people at Jane's party! But the Countdown Clock had not stopped.

Tessa shook her head. "See? Something is wrong. But there's still time to fix it. We just have to figure out what happened."

Sage sat down and buried her head in her hands. What was going on? She had done everything right!

"I don't get it," she said. "My necklace lit up when I met Jane."

"Do you think that she had another wish?" Tessa asked.

"No," replied Sage. "She told me this was her heart's desire."

Tessa wrinkled her brow. "Maybe your Wish Pendant malfunctioned?"

Sage took a deep breath. Her mind began to race. The pendant had glowed when she met Jane, hadn't it? She replayed the scene in her mind. She met Jane, stepped back to look at the glowing pendant—and bumped into Genevieve.

Oh, starf. Genevieve, the girl whom she had sprayed with an entire container of chocolate milk, the girl who totally disliked her, the one girl who was not invited to the party, was her Wisher.

Sage stood up and walked to the door.

"Where are you going?" Tessa asked.

Sage shook her head. "There's not enough time to explain! But I think I know how to fix this. I'll be right back!" She raced outside to find Jane, who was grinning, her cheeks flushed pink with excitement and happiness.

Sage ran to the front gate, throwing it open and nearly knocking over one of Jane's guests in the process.

She had wasted all her wish energy on the wrong wish. She couldn't even rely on her secret talent to help make this wish come true. She was all on her own. And she literally didn't have a starmin—make that a second—to lose.

CHAPTER
12

Please be home, *please be home, please be home,*
Sage thought as she rang the bell for the third time.
To her great relief, the door swung open. There stood
Genevieve. She did not look pleased at all to see Sage.
She crossed her arms, her golden bracelets jangling.

"What do you want?" Genevieve asked crossly.

"I want you to come to Jane's party," Sage said. "And
so does she." She smiled. She suddenly felt much better
just standing next to Genevieve.

Genevieve's eyes lit up for a brief moment, but then
she frowned. "Well, I don't," she retorted, starting to
close the door.

Sage stuck out her foot to hold it open. Genevieve

looked very annoyed. "It's a little late, don't you think?" she asked.

"It was a mistake," explained Sage.

Genevieve laughed bitterly. "Don't you get it? I'm never invited to anything. For some crazy reason, everyone thinks I'm mean. And here's the funny part: I'm not even sure how that started.

"I'm not mean at all," she explained. "Maybe girls are jealous that I live in this big house or because I have fancy clothes. I don't know. But somehow the rumor got started that I'm mean. And I'm not," Genevieve repeated.

Her shoulders sagged. "I'm actually really nice."

She pointed to the shirt Sage was wearing. "Like when I came over in the cafeteria to tell you I liked your tie-dyed shirts. And everyone assumed I was just being sarcastic. And then you ruined my dress."

"I'm sorry," said Sage. "That was an accident." Then she realized something. "Hey, you really like the shirts?"

"Yeah," Genevieve said. "They're really pretty. They just need a little flash."

"That's what Jane was saying!" cried Sage. "Come on, you're the most fashionable girl in the class. What do you think the shirts need?"

"I'm the most fashionable girl in the *school*,"

Genevieve said with a smile. She studied the shirt. "I think it needs rhinestones." She reached forward and touched one of Sage's sleeves. "I also think you could decorate the sleeves. You know, gather them and tie them up with pretty satin ribbons."

Sage nodded excitedly. "Jane is going to love it," she said.

"I can lend you some ribbon and a rhinestone machine," said Genevieve.

Sage blinked in disbelief. Genevieve really *was* nice! "Actually," said Sage, "I was hoping you could bring them to the party. To show everyone how to use them." Genevieve paused for a moment. She bit her lip, sucked in her cheeks, and crossed her arms.

"You wish people would realize that you really are a nice person," guessed Sage. Oh, how she could've used her mind-reading skill just then! "Then you would be invited to birthday parties. Like Jane's." Genevieve looked embarrassed.

Sage jumped as a zap of electric current raced down her spine. It was like Professor Lucretia Delphinus had described, only much more intense.

"Are you okay?" asked Genevieve.

Sage nodded briskly. She did her best to collect

herself and said, "I can't think of anything nicer than helping someone out at their birthday party."

Genevieve still didn't look convinced.

Sage grabbed her hand. "Humor me, Genevieve," she said. "And repeat after me: I believe in you. Glow for it!"

Genevieve rolled her eyes. "What? That's crazy!"

"Please?" said Sage. She grabbed Genevieve's other hand, and together they repeated the words.

And then it happened: Sage felt a warm glow course through her, going out her right hand. She saw Genevieve smile as the surge of energy flowed through her and back to Sage's left hand. Genevieve had no idea what had just happened, but Sage had a wonderful feeling of peace and contentment. It was almost as if she was floating—though when she looked down she saw her feet firmly planted on the floor.

"Okay," said Genevieve. "Let's do this." She ran upstairs. Sage had a couple of nerve-racking moments as she watched the starmins tick by on her Countdown Clock.

But before too long, Genevieve came back downstairs wearing a pretty blue party dress and her golden bangles, a tote bag slung over her shoulder. "I've got everything we need," she said. "Let's go!"

They got back to Jane's house quickly. Genevieve suddenly grew shy as they pushed open the gate and walked to the backyard. Sage couldn't really blame her for feeling self-conscious as all eyes turned to her and the party grew quiet.

"Maybe I should just go back . . ." started Genevieve.

It didn't help when Jenna broke the silence. "Well, look who's here," she said. "Ms. Meanie herself."

But then Jane pushed forward, looking a little worried. "Hi, Genevieve," she said. "I'm glad you came to my party."

Genevieve bit her lip nervously. "Thanks for inviting me," she said. "I'm sorry I don't have a present. But I did bring these." She pulled out the rhinestone machine, containers full of sparkling stones, and thin satiny ribbons in every color of the rainbow. She grabbed an almost-dry T-shirt, and with a few lengths of ribbon and some artfully placed rhinestones, she transformed it from cute to completely dazzling.

"I want to do that!" Madison cried. Soon all the girls were clamoring for Genevieve's help. Even Jenna wanted to try it.

Jane smiled at Sage. "Wow, that's exactly what I was hoping for!"

Tessa walked over, a glass of lemonade in her hand. She had a funny grin on her face. "This stuff is goooooood," she said. She hiccupped. "But the clock is still ticking. You are almost out of time." She giggled. "Out of time!' she repeated.

Sage stared at Tessa. What was wrong with her? Then she looked at her Countdown Clock. Two starmins to go—and counting.

Her heart sank. Tessa was right. Time had run out for her.

CHAPTER
13

Just then she heard Jenna's voice. "Maybe I was wrong," she said. "Genevieve, you're actually pretty nice after all."

Genevieve grinned. "You're not so bad yourself, Jenna."

"Tessa look!" Sage cried. Tessa grabbed Sage's hand. Before Sage's amazed eyes, positive wish energy began to pour out of Genevieve, who had no idea that anything was happening. It danced through the air in a beautiful rainbow-colored arc before being absorbed into Sage's Wish Pendant.

And that's when the Countdown Clock stopped.

WISH GRANTED: MISSION COMPLETE, the Star-Zap screen read.

And then: COME HOME!

Tessa jumped up and down and hugged Sage. "I can't believe it! You did it!" she shouted. "This calls for some more lemonade."

Ella laughed. "Wow," she said. "Sage's friend *really* likes tie-dye."

Just then Mrs. Newman came up to Sage and placed a hand on her arm. "Thank you for making my daughter's birthday wish come true," she told her.

"You're very welcome," replied Sage. If Mrs. Newman only knew the half of it!

Tessa and Sage stayed until just after the birthday cake was unveiled. Because how could a Star Darling miss seeing a real live Wishling birthday cake? Everyone gasped when they saw the colorful confection—tie-dyed frosting on the outside and vibrant tie-dyed cake on the inside. Instead of candles, a profusion of sparklers rose from the center, shooting out a cascade of shimmering sparks. Everyone sang except for the Star Darlings; they didn't know the words. "I don't have to make a wish," Jane said as the cake was placed in front of her. "I got just what I wanted." She smiled at Sage. "Thank you, Sage."

"Oh, make one anyway," suggested Sage. "You can never have enough wishes. Good wishes, that is," she hastily added.

"I'll see you at home," Tessa told Sage when she had finished her third glass of lemonade. "This stuff is sooooooo
good!" she said. She gave Sage a big hug, then grabbed her
shoulders and looked deeply into her eyes. "Now it's time
for you to say good-bye to Jane and Genevieve."

Sage gulped. How she hated good-byes! She had
known this was coming, but it still was not going to
be easy. Even though she hadn't really been assigned to
Jane, she was still going to miss her. And Genevieve—
she would never forget her first Wisher. Ever.

Sage found Jane and Genevieve together, chatting
like old friends.

"I need to talk to you two," Sage told them. "In private."

The three girls walked to the front yard. Sage took
a deep breath, anxiously poking at a balloon from the
bunch tied to the fence. Jane's cheeks were flushed with
excitement. "I can't believe it!" she gushed. "What a great
party! Genevieve really made the shirts look awesome."
She added, "We're going to go shopping together tomorrow; isn't that great?"

Genevieve smiled. "And we were both invited to
Jenna's sleepover next weekend."

Sage smiled. Genevieve's wish was so powerful
and so pure because it hadn't just involved her—it had
affected everyone else at the party.

"By sharing yourself and your talents with everyone today, you made yourself happy, but you also brought joy to others, Genevieve," Sage told her. "Now you have to remember to take that happiness and hold on to it. You can close your eyes whenever you want and visualize your wish coming true. And feel that same happiness all over again."

The two girls looked at each other and nodded. "Thank you, Sage. You made both our wishes come true today," Genevieve said.

"Yeah, everyone is saying that this is the most fun party ever . . ." Jane's voice softened. "Sage, why do you look so sad?"

"I've got to go," Sage said, her voice thick. She was unable to meet Jane's gaze. "It has been great getting to know you guys and . . ."

Then her voice trailed off. But she had an idea. It went against everything she had been warned about. However, it just felt right. Summoning her energy, she held her Wish Pendant tightly in her hand and recited: "Star light, star bright, the first star I see tonight: I wish I may, I wish I might, have the wish I wish tonight."

Jane and Genevieve looked at her oddly, but their expressions quickly changed to ones of amazement.

A warm glow came over her, and Sage could feel it

coursing through her body, from the ends of her braids to the very tips of her toes. She glanced down at her now-lavender hair and admired her skin, which was glimmering once more. Jane and Genevieve just stared, their eyes wide, almost entranced. "Oh, Sage," Jane breathed. "You're so beautiful!"

Jane reached over and touched Sage's hair. "Your hair is lavender! And your skin is so sparkly!"

Genevieve shook her head. "How in the world?"

Without thinking, Sage leaned forward and gave first Jane and then Genevieve a tight squeeze. When she stepped back, she had returned to her dull Wishling appearance. The two girls stared at her blankly.

"Are you two okay?" Sage asked them.

The girls both had curious but distant looks on their faces. "Excuse me," Jane said, "but do I know you?" She smiled politely, waiting for an answer.

"Yeah," said Genevieve. "Have we met before?"

Sage blinked. It looked like her good-bye hug had completely wiped the girls' memories!

"No," she managed to say. "You don't know me at all." She took a deep breath.

"I just wanted to wish you a very happy birthday, Jane."

Epilogue

Moments after Sage had arrived back on Starland, her Star-Zap buzzed. REPORT TO WISH-HOUSE OFFICE IMMEDIATELY.

Sage knew she had come so close to failing her Wish Mission. Was she going to get into trouble? Would she be kicked off the Star Darlings team? Was it proof that Vivica was right, that she was never supposed to be at Starling Academy in the first place? Her stomach was in knots with worry, even though everything had turned out okay at the end.

Still, despite her nervousness, a feeling of peace came over Sage as she walked down the hallways of Starling Academy. Sage hadn't realized just how much she had missed Starland. She felt safe and welcome, waving to classmates who had no idea who she was. Or that she'd been gone at all. It didn't matter. She was just happy to be back, no matter what the consequences.

"Miss Sage!" said a funny voice.

Sage looked around the empty hallway. Was she hearing things?

"Up here!" said the voice.

Sage looked up. A small Bot-Bot guide hovered near the ceiling.

"It's me! MO-J4!"

"Oh, hey," said Sage, trying to remember if they had met before.

"I gave you a tour of the campus!" said MO-J4 a little peevishly. "So where have you been?"

"Oh, around," said Sage vaguely. She reached Lady Stella's door and knocked.

"Come in," said Lady Stella.

Sage concentrated and the door slid open silently.

"Nicely done," said MO-J4 admiringly. "I'll see you around, Miss Sage."

"See you," said Sage.

Pushing open the door, Sage spotted the other eleven Star Darlings seated around the table, all studying her curiously—except for Cassie, who gave her a wave and a huge grin.

"Welcome home, Sage," said the headmistress. "Congratulations on a successful mission."

And then all her fellow Star Darlings gave Sage a standing ovation.

"Really?" said Sage incredulously. "But I almost totally messed up!"

Lady Stella shook her head. "Sage, what you did was incredibly brave. You went on a mission to an unfamiliar world. Of course there were going to be glitches!" She smiled.

Sage breathed a sigh of relief. "Star salutations," she said. "But I want to thank Tessa for coming down to help me out."

"You fixed it all by yourself," said Tessa.

The headmistress held the Wish Orb and beckoned Sage to come closer, then solemnly placed it in her hands.

Sage held the Wish Orb in her hands. Its glow became more and more intense. "Look!" said Vega. "Something is happening!" To Sage's delight, the orb began to transform into a lavender boheminella, a luminous flower whose head hung like a lantern from its stem. It glowed with a soft light, and stardust drifted down from the blossom in a delicate cascade. "It's beautiful!" Sage breathed. "It is," agreed Lady Stella. "And from now on, this will be your personal Wish Blossom." Suddenly, the petals of the flower began to tremble. What was going on? Sage gasped as the flower opened to reveal a glossy dark purple stone with deep veins of shimmering starlight. It looked like a mini galaxy was locked inside its gleaming surface. Sage felt a deep sense of peace and well-being.

"Well, that is most extraordinary!" said Lady Stella, shaking her head.

"What is it?" Sage asked as the Star Darlings pressed closer to see the shimmering stone.

"All in due time," said Lady Stella. Sage thought the headmistress looked surprised—pleasantly so. "Until then, please guard this precious stone with your very life."

Sage took a deep breath and looked around the room at her fellow Star Darlings, enjoying her moment in the spotlight.

And she wondered which one of them would be next.

Sage lingered in Lady Stella's office after the room had cleared.

"Can I help you with anything, Sage?" Lady Stella asked kindly.

"I was wondering . . . I heard that maybe . . . I mean that someone told me . . ." Sage hemmed and hawed, unable to ask the headmistress the difficult question.

"The answer is no, Sage," Lady Stella answered. "You were admitted on your own strengths. No one helped you."

Sage grinned. "Star salutations, Lady Stella," was all she could say. "Star salutations."

Sage still couldn't shake the feeling that there was a look of concern on Lady Stella's face. And she hoped that she hadn't disappointed her in any way. But Sage practically skipped the whole way back to her room. She placed her hand on the scanner and it glowed bright blue. "Welcome home, Sage," the voice said. "And congratulations on a job well done!"

Sage stepped inside. Cassie was standing in front of her closet, a strange look on her face.

Sage reached into her backpack. "I brought something back for you," she said. "A Wishling book. It really is made out of paper."

Cassie gasped as Sage placed the book in her hands. "I wondered what one would look like," she said, running her fingers over the cover. She opened it and immediately started devouring the words. Then, realizing what she was doing, she laughed and closed the book, hugging it to her chest. "Wow—this is incredible. Star salutations, Sage. I'm glad you're back." Then she added shyly, "It was kind of lonely without you. I did a lot of thinking while

you were away, and there's something I have to tell you."
She fidgeted nervously.

"Do you want to tell me about your pet glowfur?"
Sage asked with a smile.

Cassie's eyes widened. "How did you . . ."

"I had some time to think about it when I was alone
on Wishworld," Sage explained. "I put it all together—
the dream I had, which wasn't really a dream, was it?
The Green Globule you ate, the glow from the closet,
the sweet music."

Cassie opened her closet door. "Don't be afraid," she
said. "You can come out." A small, furry, winged creature flew out, nuzzled Cassie's cheek, and landed on her
shoulder. It began to sing the same beautiful song that
Sage had heard, its belly glowing contentedly.

"I was afraid to tell you," Cassie said. "I wasn't sure
if you liked pets."

"I do," said Sage. "Especially a cute one like this.
What's his—or is it her—name?"

"Bitty," said Cassie, blushing. "She was my mom's
when she was little," she explained. Cassie lowered her
eyes. "She really means a lot to me. Are you sure you're
okay with this? Starling Academy has a no-pet policy,
you know."

"It does?" said Sage.

"It's in the Student Manual," Cassie explained. At Sage's blank look she added, "You said you read it!"

"I must have skipped that part," said Sage.

Cassie giggled as the glowfur took off and landed on her head. "I hate to break the rules, but I'm so homesick, and Bitty would be miserable without me." She smiled at her roommate. "I'm so glad you know. You can take care of her when it's time for my mission!"

"Absolutely," Sage said with a yawn. She got herself ready for bed in record time and slipped underneath the covers.

"So, tell me all about it," Cassie said, her eyes shining. "Everything that happened. What the girls were like. Exactly what the wish was. What kind of clothes did they wear? Everything!"

The glowfur began her evening song. It was sweet and gentle and calming. Sage yawned and began to speak. "It was a pretty bumpy ride down to Wishworld. I landed on a hill in the middle of a park and . . ." and then Sage fell asleep midsentence.

Her story would have to wait until tomorrow.

Glossary

Afterglow: When Starlings die, it is said that they have "begun their afterglow."

Age of Fulfillment: The age when a Starling is considered mature enough to begin studying wish granting.

Bad Wish Orbs: Orbs that are from cruel or selfish wishes. They are quickly sent to the special containment center.

Band Shell: A covered stage located in the Star Quad.

Big Dipper Dormitory: Where third- and fourth-year students live.

Bit Bat: a creature that lives underground in the Star Caves.

Boheminella: A luminous lavender flower. Boheminella is Sage's personal Wish Blossom.

Booshel Bay: A vacation destination.

Bot-Bot: A Starland robot. There are Bot-Bot guards, waiters, deliverers, and guides on Starland.

Bright Day: The date a Starling is born, celebrated each year like Wishling birthdays.

Celestial Café: Starling Academy's outstanding cafeteria.

Cosmic Transporter: The moving sidewalk system at Starling Academy that transports students through dorms and across campus.

Countdown Clock: A timer that lets a Starling know how much time she has left to complete her Wish Mission, it coincides with when the Wish Orb will fade.

Crystal Mountains: The most beautiful mountains on Starland; located across the lake from Starling Academy.

Cyber Journal: Where the Star Darlings record their Wishworld observations.

Cybernetics Lab: Where Bot-Bots are built.

Cyber-wrestlers: Popular children's toys that battle each other.

Festival of Illumination: A celebration of lights and family that comes midway through the Time of Shadows.

Flash Vertical Mover: A mode of transportation similar to a Wishling elevator, only superfast.

Floozel: Starland equivalent of a Wishworld mile.

Flutterfocus: A Starland creature similar to a Wishworld butterfly with illuminated wings.

Galliope: A Starland creature similar to a sparkly Wishworld horse.

Garble greens: A Starland vegetable similar to spinach.

Glamera: A holographic image-recording device.

Glion: A gentle Starland creature similar in appearance to a Wishworld lion, but with a multicolored glowing mane.

Globerbeem: A Starland creature similar to a Wishworld lightning bug, only more sparkly.

Glorange: A glowing orange fruit, its juice is often enjoyed at breakfast.

Glowfur: A small, furry Starland creature with gossamer wings that eats flowers and glows.

Glowin' Glions: Starling Academy's top-ranked star ball team.

Good Wish Orbs: Positive and helpful wishes that come from the heart.

Green Globules: Green pellets that are fed to pet glowfurs. They don't taste very good to Starlings.

Halo Hall: The building where Starling Academy classes are held.

Holo-book: Starling books; the pages are projected into the air.

Holo-paper: Starling newspapers; the pages are projected into the air.

Holo-place card: Projections used around tables to indicate where Starlings should sit.

Illumination Library: The impressive library at Starling Academy.

Impossible Wish Orbs: Wishes that are beyond the power of Starlings to grant.

Iridusvapor: A gas found on Starland, it makes Kaleidoscope trees change color.

Kaleidoscope tree: A rare and beautiful tree whose blossoms continuously change color.

Keytar: An instrument that is held like a guitar but has keys instead of strings.

Light Giving Day: A holiday held on the first day of the Time of New Beginnings. It celebrates renewal and the return of warmer weather.

Lightning Lounge: A place on the Starling Academy campus where students relax and socialize.

Little Dipper Dormitory: Where Sage lives. All first- and second-year students live in this dorm.

Luminous Lake: A serene and lovely lake next to the Starling Academy campus.

Mirror Mantra: A saying specific to each Star Darling that gives her and her Wisher reassurance and strength. When a Starling recites her Mirror Mantra while looking into a mirror on Wishworld, she will see her true appearance reflected back.

Moonberry: A fruit that is a lot like a blueberry, but with a more intense flavor. Sage hates them.

Moonium: Equivalent of a Wishworld million.

Old Prism: A medium-sized historical city about an hour from Starling Academy.

Power Crystal: The powerful stone that each Star Darling receives once she has granted her first wish.

Radiant Recreation Center: Starling Academy's fitness and sports center.

Rodangular: A beautiful bright pink stone.

Safety starglasses: Worn by Starlings to protect their eyes when in close proximity to a shooting star.

Serenity Gardens: Extensive botanical gardens set on an island in Luminous Lake.

Shooting stars: Speeding stars that Starlings can latch on to and ride to Wishworld.

Silver Blossom: The final manifestation of a Good Wish Orb, this glimmering metallic bloom is placed in the Hall of Granted Wishes.

Sparkle shower: An energy shower Starlings take every day to get clean and refresh their sparkling glow.

Star ball: An intramural sport that shares similarities with soccer on Wishworld. But star ball players use energy manipulation to control the ball.

Starcake: A Starling breakfast item, similar to a star-shaped Wishworld pancake.

Starcar: The primary mode of transportation for most Starlings. These ultrasafe vehicles drive themselves on cushions of wish energy.

Star Caves: The secret caverns underneath Starling Academy where the Star Darlings' secret Wish-Cavern is located.

Star Darlings: The twelve Star-Charmed Starlings chosen by Lady Stella to go on top secret missions to Wishworld.

Starday: A period of twenty-four hours on Starland, the equivalent of a Wishworld day.

Starkin: The Starling word for siblings.

Starland: An irregularly shaped world veiled by a bright yellow glow that, from a distance, makes it look like a regular star.

Starland City: The largest city on Starland is also its capital.

Starling Academy: The most prestigious all-girl four-year boarding school for wish granting on Starland.

Starlings: The glowing beings with sparkly skin that live on Starland.

Starmin: Sixty starsecs (or seconds) on Starland, the equivalent of a Wishworld minute.

Star Preparatory: Similar to Starling Academy, this is the all-boys school located across Luminous Lake.

Star Quad: The central outdoor part of the Starling Academy campus.

Star salutations: The Starling equivalent of "thank you."

Starsec: Brief period of time on Starland, similar to a Wishworld second.

Starshine Day: A Starling holiday that is held on the warmest starday during the Time of Lumiere.

Star Wranglers: Starlings whose job it is to lasso a shooting star to transport Starlings to Wishworld.

Staryear: A period of 365 days on Starland, the equivalent of a Wishworld year.

Star-Zap: The ultimate smartphone that Starlings use for all communications. It has myriad features.

Stellar Falls: The stunning waterfall that cascades into Luminous Lake.

Stinkberry: A fruit with a terrible odor.

Student Manual: A holo-book that contains all the rules and regulations of Starling Academy.

Time of Letting Go: One of the four seasons on Starland. It falls between the warmest season and the coldest, similar to fall on Wishworld.

Time of Lumiere: The warmest season on Starland, similar to summer on Wishworld.

Time of New Beginnings: Similar to spring on Wishworld, this is the season that follows the coldest time of year; it's when plants and trees come into bloom.

Time of Shadows: The coldest season of the year on Starland, similar to winter on Wishworld.

Toothlight: A high-tech gadget that Starlings use to clean their teeth.

Wee Constellation School: The Starland equivalent of preschool.

Wish Blossom: The bloom that appears from a Wish Orb after its wish is granted.

Wish Catcher: A Starling who receives Wish Orbs when they first arrive and determines what kind of wish each contains.

Wishers: The specific Wishlings that Starlings come to help.

Wish energy: The positive energy that is released when a wish is granted. Wish energy powers everything on Starland.

Wish energy manipulation: The ability to mentally harness wish energy to perform physical acts like turning off lights, closing doors, etc.

Wish Giving: A celebration of gratitude for friends and family that is held after the harvest in the Time of Letting Go.

Wish-Granters: Starlings whose job it is to travel down to Wishworld to help make wishes come true and collect wish energy.

Wish-House: The place where Wish Orbs are cared for until they sparkle. Once the orb's wish is granted, it becomes a Wish Blossom.

Wishlings: The inhabitants of Wishworld.

Wish Mission: The task Starlings undertake when they travel to Wishworld to help grant a wish.

Wish Orb: The form a wish takes on Wishworld before traveling to Starland. There it will grow and sparkle when it's time to grant the wish.

Wish Pendant: A gadget that absorbs and transports wish energy, helps Starlings locate their Wishers, and contains a cloaking device.

Wish-Watcher: Starlings whose job it is to observe the Good Wish Orbs until they glow, indicating that they are ready to be granted.

Wishworld: The planet that Starland relies on for wish energy. The beings on Wishworld know it by another name: Earth.

Wishworld Outfit Selector: A program on each Star-Zap that accesses Wishworld fashions for Starlings to wear to blend in.

Wishworld Surveillance Deck: Located high above the campus, it is where Starling Academy students go to observe Wishlings through high-powered telescopes.

Zing: A traditional Starling breakfast drink, it can be enjoyed hot or iced.

Acknowledgments

It is impossible to list all of our gratitude, but we will try. Our most precious gift and greatest teacher, Halo; we love you more than there are stars in the sky . . . punashaku. To the rest of our crazy, awesome, unique tribe—thank you for teaching us to go for our dreams. Integrity. Strength. Love. Foundation. Family. Grateful. Mimi Muldoon—from your star doodling to naming our Star Darlings, your artistry, unconditional love, and inspiration is infinite. Didi Muldoon—your belief and support in us is only matched by your fierce protection and massive-hearted guidance. Gail. Queen G. Your business sense and witchy wisdom are legendary. Frank—you are missed and we know you are watching over us all. Along with Tutu, Nana, and Deda, who are always present, gently guiding us in spirit. To our colorful, totally genius, and bananas siblings—Patrick, Moon, Diva, and Dweezil—there is more creativity and humor in those four names than most people experience in a lifetime. Blessed. To our magical nieces—Mathilda, Zola, Ceylon, and Mia—the Star Darlings adore you and so do we. Our witchy cuzzie fairy godmothers—Ane and Gina. Our fairy fashion godfather, Paris. Teeta and Freddy—we love you all so much. And our four-legged fur babies—Sandwich, Luna, Figgy, and Pinky Star.

The incredible Barry Waldo. Our SD partner. Sent to us from above in perfect timing. Your expertise and friendship are beyond words. We love you and Gary to the moon and back. Long live the manifestation room!

Catherine Daly—the stars shined brightly upon us the day we aligned with you. Your talent and inspiration are otherworldly; our appreciation cannot be expressed in words. Many heartfelt hugs for you and the adorable Oonagh.

To our beloved Disney family. Thank you for believing in us. Wendy Lefkon, our master guide and friend through this entire journey. Stephanie Lurie, for being the first to believe in Star Darlings. Suzanne Murphy, who helped every step of the way. Jeanne Mosure, we fell in love with you the first time we met and Star Darlings wouldn't be what it is without you. Andrew Sugarman, thank you so much for all your support.

Our team . . . Devon (pony pants) and our Monsterfoot crew—so grateful. Richard Scheltinga—our angel and protector. Chris Abramson—thank you! Special appreciation to Richard Thompson, John LaViolette, Swanna, Mario, and Sam.

To our friends old and new—we are so grateful to be on this rad journey that is life with you all. Fay. Jorja. Chandra. Sananda. Sandy. Kathryn. Louise. What wisdom and strength you share. Ruth, Mike, and the rest of our magical Wagon Wheel bunch—how lucky we are. How inspiring you are. We love you.

Last—we have immeasurable gratitude for every person we've met along our journey, for all the good and the bad; it is all a gift. From the bottom of our hearts we thank you for touching our lives.

Don't miss

Libby and the Class Election

Available now wherever books and eBooks are sold

Next in the series

Leona's Last Chance

Vega and the Fashion Disaster

Scarlet Discovers True Strength

A Wisher's Guide to Starland

Shana Muldoon Zappa is a jewelry designer and writer who was born and raised in Los Angeles. With an endless imagination, a passion to inspire positivity through her many artistic endeavors, and her background in fashion, Shana created Star Darlings. She and her husband, Ahmet Zappa, collaborated on Star Darlings especially for their magical little girl and biggest inspiration, Halo Violetta Zappa.

Ahmet Zappa is the *New York Times* best-selling author of *Because I'm Your Dad* and *The Monstrous Memoirs of a Mighty McFearless*. He writes and produces films and television shows and loves pancakes, unicorns, and making funny faces for Halo and Shana.